MAMBO

AND

MURDER

A Fiona Quinn Mystery

By

C.S. McDonald

MAMBO AND MURDER

MAMBO

AND

MURDER

A Fiona Quinn Mystery

By

C.S. McDonald

PROLOGUE

Detective Nathan Landry slid out of his SUV and tossed a bite-size Snickers bar into his mouth. Folding his arms over his chest, he leaned against the vehicle to study the split-level home on Aljo Drive in the Upper Saint Clair neighborhood of Pittsburgh. Officer Wyatt Hays' police vehicle sat in the driveway. As a member of the homicide division of the Pittsburgh Police, Landry was stymied and somewhat annoyed at being summoned to the residence. Nonetheless, he pushed away from the SUV and made his way toward the house. When he stepped inside the home, he found Wyatt walking toward him with a clipboard in his hand. The interior of the house was stripped down—no pictures or décor hung on the walls. Only a sofa, two stuffed chairs, two end tables, and a lone lamp filled the space.

"What's going on, Wyatt? They said this house was burgled a couple days ago. I don't see a dead body, so why am *I* here?" Narrowing his eyes, he scanned the room once more—the furniture was covered in gray fingerprint powder. "Why did you dust for prints? We don't usually do that for a simple *burglary*—it's too messy."

"The homeowner's daughter insisted. You know how it is—people watch too many cop shows on TV. They think we should dust for everything. Now, she's got a big mess to clean up, but in her defense, we hit pay-dirt. We've already arrested the next-door neighbor kid," Wyatt said.

"Okay, great. You've made a quick arrest on a burglary. Again, what's that got to do with me?"

"The homeowner, Angelo Moretti, passed six months ago. When his daughter was told about the break-in, she came home and wanted to talk with a police officer—that's why I'm here. Anyway, I think you'll understand in a minute. Read the print results." He handed Detective Landry the clipboard. While the detective examined the information on the report, Wyatt explained, "The house has been empty for six months. Mr. Moretti's estate is still being hashed-out. The kid broke a bedroom window. I think he was looking for valuables to sell, but as you can see the house doesn't have much in it. We found multiple prints, but I think these are the ones you'll be most interested in—they belong to a Vincent Di Volante." He pointed to a specific spot on the page. "I would've just shown them to you at the precinct, but I figured you'd want to talk with the daughter."

Detective Landry's eyebrows arched. "The report says the prints not only belong to Di Volante, but he's been dead for over *forty years*?" He continued to read and then looked up to meet Wyatt's gaze. "And he was a suspect in *three* murders?"

"Now you're comin' around. Mr. Moretti's daughter is in the kitchen and it's right through that door. Oh, her name is Teresa Kester." Snatching the clipboard from the detective's hand, he added, "See ya later." With that, he hurried from the house.

Taking in the bare room, the detective ran his hand over the nape of his neck, then made his way into the kitchen. He found Teresa pouring a cup of coffee. Flashing his badge, he said, "Hello, Ms. Kester, I'm Detective Nathan Landry, Pittsburgh Homicide."

"*Doctor* Kester," she said then turned with a rather mystified look on her face. "Homicide? I admit I'm *upset* with the neighbor, but I certainly didn't kill him—he's in police custody. Now, I'm stuck with this clean-up and the cost of replacing a window before the house goes on the market next week." On her way to a small dinette pressed against the wall, she held up her free hand. "Not that murder didn't cross my mind."

The detective snorted. "Can't say that I blame you." He noticed a clean mug sitting on the counter next to the coffeemaker. He gestured to the mug. "Do you mind?"

"Please, help yourself and have a seat. I'm most interested in hearing why I'm talking with a homicide detective over a robbery—I don't see a dead body," the doctor put in.

He poured some coffee into the mug. "Do you know a man named, Vincent Di Volante?"

"No, I've never heard of him."

Turning, he leaned a hip against the counter. "His fingerprints are all through your father's living room. Looks like he was here often. You've never run into him?"

"That's very possible, Detective. I haven't lived in this area for twenty-two years. I'm a busy pediatrician in Seattle. Although, I've made several trips here lately—for the funeral, and to clean out the house. Otherwise, I rarely make it home. My father would visit me far more often than I visited him."

"Is your mother in the area?"

"Mom passed five years ago—lung cancer."

"I'm sorry."

"Thank you. I miss them both terribly." She took a sip of her coffee.

"So, you've been away for twenty-two years—that leaves quite a few years unaccounted for, ma'am," the detective pointed out.

"I understand what you're getting at, but I simply don't know Vincent Di Volante. Maybe he went by another name?"

"Maybe."

"So, what's the big deal with this guy? Did he kill someone? I assure you, my father wasn't much into criminals—let alone murderers."

"Mr. Di Volante is dead."

She smiled at him over her cup. "So is my father, Detective, and his prints are all over this house."

"I hear ya. Here's the thing, according to our records, Mr. Di Volante has been dead for well over forty years, and yet, his fingerprints have shown up in your father's living room."

Cocking her head to one side, the doctor furrowed her brows. "How is that possible?"

Detective Landry raised his cup as if to toast. "That's what I mean to find out."

ONE

When her eyes weren't wide with shock and her right hand wasn't cupped over her mouth, Fiona Quinn had wrapped her fingers so tightly around the seat of her chair that her knuckles had turned bright white.

She winced.

She grimaced.

She flinched.

And yes, there were moments she had to turn her face away because she could no longer bear to watch. One question kept repeating over and over again in her head, how could her dear Nathan be such a *lousy* dancer? No… scratch that. Nathan wasn't just a lousy dancer—he was downright, straight up, and without a doubt, dangerous!

Over the past forty-five minutes, she'd witnessed Nathan step on Tavia's feet, trip her, drop her, and yes, much to Fiona's and the instructor's despair, he'd elbowed her in the face—*twice*.

Okay. In Nathan's defense—Tavia wasn't exactly a graceful partner.

The ballroom dancing class Pittsburgh homicide Detective Nathan Landry and Officer Tavia Andrews were taking for a case they were about to embark upon was less of a dance class and more of an exercise in self-defense—mostly for Tavia. Hm, self-defense may not have been a vivid enough description of the scenario playing out before her—self-preservation may have been more on point—perhaps for both of them.

Tavia looked exhausted—physically and mentally.

Nathan looked embarrassed and totally defeated.

The instructor looked exasperated to the point of an acute break-down.

Yikes!

"Honestly, Fiona, I don't know how I'm going to survive this assignment. I think I'd rather face a bank robber with his gun drawn, accompanied by a rabid Pit Bull, in a dark alley than another ballroom dancing class with Nathan," Tavia had told her several days ago over pastries and coffee at De Fer Coffee and Tea on Smallman Street in the Strip District of Pittsburgh.

Truly believing Tavia had to be exaggerating, Fiona asked, "C'mon, how bad can he possibly be?"

A nanosecond after Fiona's question spilled from her lips, Tavia yanked up the leg of her jeans to show-off the black, blue, and yellow with a hint of purple bruise on her shin. "This…" Tavia began, "…is compliments of one, Detective Nathan Landry. I'm serious, Fiona, for your own well-being, I'd skip the bridal dance at your wedding. Well, if you should ever decide to marry Nate."

Fiona couldn't be certain, but Tavia must've noticed a hint of doubt in her expression. So, she added, "Hey, we've got a class on Thursday if you're looking for proof."

Hence, Fiona's current attendance at the ballroom dancing studio in Monroeville.

"All right, all right!" The instructor called out, actually, it was more like a desperate shriek, bringing Fiona back to the moment. "I think we've had quite enough for today—or at least I have."

Now, Fiona had attended many dance classes in her life, yet she had no memory of an instructor appearing as flushed with agitation as this young woman.

"Are you sure?" Nathan asked. "We haven't been practicing for very long. Shouldn't we go over change of position with Tavia turning a couple more times?"

"No!" Both Tavia and the instructor exclaimed in unison.

"Oh…okay…well, maybe we can start out with that tomorrow," Nathan suggested.

"Or maybe I'll get lucky and take a bullet tonight during my shift," Tavia grumbled as she limped toward her duffle bag lying near the door. She stuffed her dance shoes into the bag, pushed her feet into a pair of flip-flops, flung the duffle over her shoulder, and without so much as a see ya later or even a nod, she marched out of the studio.

Wow.

Fiona did not see the instructor leave the studio area, but she was suddenly nowhere to be found. Nathan plopped down in the chair next to her with a loud grunt.

Yes, it was the worst dancing she'd ever witnessed, but Fiona felt the need to be as supportive as possible. "That went well, I thought."

He tossed her a baleful look. "I'm not twelve—you don't need to patronize me."

"Okay…it was perfectly awful."

"Don't I know it. What are we gonna do? Our assignment is coming up really quickly—we've got to be good, or at least somewhat in sync. We're just not meshing."

"Not *meshing*? It looks like you're trying to kill Tavia to the beat of the music—kind of. I'm not sure either of you took one step in rhythm with the music. I'm not sure either of you—"

"I get it. I get it. We're terrible. I'm not sure which one of us the instructor hates worse, me or Tav," he said, pulling his dance shoes from his feet then pitching them to the floor in disgust.

"What's the instructor's name?" Fiona asked.

"Angelina Ballerina."

Now it was Fiona who was tossing the baleful look. "That can't be right. How do you know about Angelina Ballerina anyway?"

"Angela Rivetti, but I was close. You're a kindergarten teacher, I hear those silly names often enough and I pay attention—it's kinda my job. I should check to see if she has a rap sheet," Nathan groused.

"The *instructor*?"

"Yep."

"Why?"

"Meh, she acts like someone who'd have a rap sheet," Nathan mumbled.

"Mr. Baumbacher…" Angela called from behind.

Fiona and Nathan turned. He replied, "Yes, Ms. Angela?"

She strode toward them with a most vehement grimace on her face, while patting her neck with a towel. "I think you should know that you and your cousin… what's her name again?"

"Billie Jean…Billie Jean Baumbacher," Nathan supplied.

The instructor's grimace turned more toward a solid scowl. "Yes, Billie Jean, anyway, I think the two of you are either going to end up famous or infamous. Nonetheless, in my opinion, you are wasting your money. Where you and your cousin ever got the notion that you could compete in the Glass Slipper Ballroom Competition in the coming weeks, I will never know, but I can assure you that you cannot be ready in time. This will be *my* first time at the competition, my boyfriend's as well—and we're *good*. No. It's simply *impossible* to prepare the two of you in such a short amount of time—with such a short amount of talent."

"I—" Nathan began.

Ms. Angela whipped her hand up in a halting fashion while looking Fiona up and down. "Who is this?"

"Um…she's our other cousin…Fi…Felica," Nathan said.

The woman's eyes went to Nathan's thick nest of dark hair, and then to Fiona's strawberry blonde locks. "She doesn't look like she could be your cousin—neither does the other one for that matter."

"Both are from my mother's side—my mom's Irish."

"Okay, listen, Mr. *Astaire*, I've just talked to the owner of the studio. You have two more classes for which you have paid—after that, *we're done*." She spun on her dancing shoes, tossed her hands in the air to indicate the conversation was over, and stomped out of the room, slamming the door.

Fiona groused, "I agree. She does seem like someone who'd have a rap sheet. C'mon, let's get out of here. I'll make you some of my famous marmalade chicken."

"Now, *that's* the best offer I've had all day." He took Fiona by the hand, picked up his shoes, and they made their way toward the exit.

"Billie Jean Baumbacher? Really? I'm almost afraid to ask, but what is *your* name in this whole sham?"

"Walter—Walter Baumbacher at your service," Nathan replied.

She rolled her eyes. "No wonder you can't dance—I don't think I'd be able to perform with names like *those*." He held the door open for her, and as she stepped outside, she added wryly, "So, your mom's Irish?"

"Yeah—who knew?"

The traffic on the Parkway was fairly light. The Fort Pitt Tunnels weren't barraged with the usual back-ups, so Fiona and Nathan made the drive from Monroeville to Westwood in rather good time. Fiona had left the windows down in her blue and white Mini Cooper, allowing the warm evening breeze to waft through the car, lifting her hair from her shoulders. Nathan laid his head against the headrest with his eyes closed.

"So…what is this case you and Tavia are assigned to—you've never said."

15

Keeping his eyes closed, Nathan murmured, "I can't tell you."

"Why not?"

"Cuz then I'd have to kill you."

"Very funny."

"Actually, it's a case from about forty years ago that the department closed and has now reopened. The basic gist is, way back when, several ballroom dancers were murdered, and the suspect whom they thought was dead has resurfaced in the area. We think he may still be involved in the ballroom dance circuits, and we're thinking he may show up at the Glass Slipper Competition Miss Angela mentioned. That's why Tav and I are learning how to dance—or should I say, *trying* to learn," Nathan explained.

"Wow. They thought the murderer was dead, and now he's not? How does *that* work?"

"I'm still gathering all the information on the case, but I believe we may have a case of mistaken identity—on the part of our *dead* suspect. We'll see," Nathan explained.

"So, you're basically saying that the dead guy may not be the right person?"

"Yep."

"Your dead suspect who is now alive, has to be pretty old, doesn't he?"

"He should be in his early seventies, yes. But just because these murders happened a long time ago doesn't make it less wrong, does it? Just because a murderer is elderly doesn't mean he or she should simply be excused, does it?"

"Absolutely not. Where were the dancers murdered?"

"From what I've been able to gather so far, they were murdered several months apart—each one was found in a men's room after a ballroom competition—at different locations. All three had been shot."

"Wow. They all died the same way—in a *men's* room? That's really bold. You'd think people attending the competition would have heard the gunshots or saw them going into the restroom."

"These ballroom events are usually held at large venues, like the David Lawrence Convention Center, downtown. I'm sure the murderer found a remote bathroom to do away with his victims," Nathan said.

"And this killer was killed, but actually may still be living. You have to admit, it sounds intriguing," Fiona put in.

"Yeah, well it won't be very *intriguing* if Tavia and I don't get our *act* together—pun *intended*," Nathan stated.

Around a chuckle, Fiona rolled the Cooper to a stop in front of her house. Slipping out of the car, she said, "It also sounds like you have to find another dance instructor, and soon. Maybe you could come up with better alias' for your next victim—" She let a giggle tumble out. "I mean, teacher."

Making their way up the sidewalk toward the house, Fiona could see Nathan was considering his options. Pulling the screen open, she held it with her hip while turning the key in the front door lock. Fiona's little white Maltese, Harriet, barked her impatience from the confines of her kennel just inside the door. When the door opened, Fiona bent down to scoop up the scattered mail from the floor that the mailman had pushed through the mail slot at some point during the day. She opened the kennel gate while Nathan held the front door open for Harriet to scoot outside and off the porch. Fiona sifted through the handful of envelopes, stopping to examine a somewhat wrinkled and slightly discolored square envelope.

Tossing the other pieces of mail onto the top of Harriet's kennel, she muttered, "What's this?"

Nathan moved closer to peer over her shoulder. "Whoa, that looks like a really old piece of mail."

"Yeah, and look, it's addressed to my grandmother from her sister, Lucille. How can that be? Both have been dead for a long time. Lucille died long before my grandmother did and look at this—the postmark is dated, December 1975." She turned the envelope over in her hands.

"Was this Lucille older or younger than your grandmother?"

"I don't remember. Actually, I'm not sure I ever knew."

"By the shape of the envelope, it looks like a Christmas card," Nathan said.

"Yes, it really does, doesn't it? Which by the date on the postmark, that's pretty much a given."

"Talk about *snail mail*—this is ridiculous. Look at the postmark, it reads, Dixmont State Hospital," Nathan pointed out.

"Hm, back in the day, their mailroom must've had their very own postmark. Interesting."

"Are you gonna open it?" Nathan asked.

Tapping the envelope against her fingers, she looked around the foyer. "I…I guess I should. Don't you think? After all, both parties are deceased. I suppose someone should open it." She stared at the strange piece of wayward mail.

"Well…go ahead…open it. Let's have a look-see," Nathan urged.

Fiona ran her finger under the flap allowing the old glue to release quite easily. The envelope popped open revealing a Christmas card that definitely came from the 1960's. The illustration on the card would be considered retro nowadays but very up to date back then. A sprig of holly swept over the top right corner of the card while a snowman with a red and white checkered scarf held a wreath in one arm and a gift in the other. The colors and graphics were a bit faded from time gone by.

"I'm no expert on Christmas cards or any other kind for that matter, but that is one old lookin' card," Nathan noted.

Fiona brushed the pads of her fingers over the card. "It sure is." She opened the card to read the greeting. "Christmas greetings and all good wishes for happiness in the coming year. It's signed, Love, Lucille, Ed, and children."

"Ed was her husband, I'm guessing," Nathan put in as he opened the door to allow Harriet back into the house.

"Hm, I suppose. I don't know very much about great Aunt Lucille. Grandma didn't speak of her very often, but it makes sense that Ed would be her husband the way the card is signed. In fact, I think Grandma raised her son, Dick, for several years after Lucille's passing."

"What happened to her?"

Fiona closed the card and held it to her chest. "I'm not sure. I do kind of remember having one brief conversation with Gram about her, and if I remember correctly, Lucille was committed and died in Dixmont."

"That was the old mental institution that was torn down in the 1980's?"

"Yep."

"Well, that definitely explains the postmark. So, what're you gonna do with the card?" Nathan inquired.

Pitching him a svelte smile, she took his hand. "C'mon, I'll show you what I'm going to do with it." She led him up the staircase with Harriet on their heels. When they got to the second floor of the house Fiona led him through the small foyer, then she opened a door revealing the stairwell that had an old stairlift attached to the wall. The staircase led to an attic apartment on the third floor where her grandmother, Evelyn Burrell, had lived while Fiona was growing up.

Fiona turned on the light in the stairwell.

Harriet scurried up the stairs ahead of them to plop down on the top step and look down on them as if asking, what's taking you so long?

Nathan looked up the stairs. "Ah, the infamous Grandma Ev apartment,"

Fiona snorted. "Infamous, like you?"

"Well, not quite. Actually, I consider myself more notorious than infamous. Why are we going up there?"

"You'll see," Fiona whispered.

He followed her up the creaky stairs. The closer they got to the top the heat became more intense and the air stale.

"You should open one or two of the windows up here for better air flow. It's always as hot as Hades up here."

"In the winter it's freezing, but I don't want to heat it or cool this area—my electric bills are high enough, thank you. But, you might be right, maybe I should open them just a bit."

When they reached the apartment, she turned on a light to illuminate the large open space that seemed to be stuck in time. White sheets had been tossed over the sofa and a winged back chair. An analog TV was stationed on a stand and old-fashioned glass candy dishes sat on the coffee table. A double bed, covered with a blue chenille bedspread, stood against the far wall, which Harriet jumped up on and stood in the middle of, wagging her tail merrily. At either side of the bed set, two dormers, each with a long window, looked out over the neighbor's house below. Near the window inside the dormer to the right, sat an old desk. A blue princess style telephone, most likely from the late 70s or early 80s, was stationed on the corner of the desk. Gold picture frames sat upon the long edge displaying images of both Fiona and her younger brother, Chad. Fiona was about fifteen in her photo and Chad about twelve. The pictures were school portraits, so they were more like mug-shots than actual portraits. Other photos were positioned about the room in the same style of gold frames—all of which were covered in a thin layer of dust. Nathan went to a window that looked out over Oxford Street, unlocked it, and opened it just a crack.

Fiona immediately went to the desk, pulled open the middle drawer, and then turned to urge Nathan to join her at the desk. Picking up a pile of cards from the drawer, she took account of each as she presented them. "Grandma always kept Christmas cards from those who were older or perhaps ill. Like this one, for example, was the last card she'd received from her older sister, Alberta." She carefully returned the card to the drawer. "This one was the last from her older sister, Anna. And this one was from her brother, Sam. This one was the last from her brother, Bob and his wife, Anna Marie. See? She hand-wrote the date up in the corner of each card."

Nathan lifted a shoulder. "She sure has a pile there. So, what's your point?"

Placing the pile back into the drawer, she laid the card from her great-aunt Lucille gently on the top and closed the drawer. "My point is, I have to assume that this card was the last she'd received from Lucille. So, I'm putting it in its proper place among the rest. I think Gram would've wanted it that way."

Nathan glanced around the apartment. "I understand where you're coming from, Fiona. But she's dead, isn't she? I don't mean to be insensitive, really, I don't, but what difference does it make where the card goes now? Unless…you're saying she's still here…in the house…is that what this is about?"

Fiona stilled. She bit her lip.

Yikes.

"C'mon, I've seen some pretty weird things go on in this house. The lights go on and off at will, and no, I don't believe for one minute it's because of the old wiring in the house. I've had a candy dish move away from my reach, and sometimes when I put something in one place, it ends up in another. So, I guess I'm asking you if there's a spirit living in your house—the spirit of your grandma Ev maybe?"

Double yikes.

Fact was, he'd hit the nail directly on the proverbial head. After her grandmother passed away, she stayed in the house to watch over Fiona and her family. Fiona loved her childhood home and she was always aware of Grandma Ev's presence. When her parents decided to retire from their teaching positions and move to Daytona, Florida, she bought the old drafty house on Oxford Street from them—with Grandma Evelyn's spirit still residing in the attic apartment.

Grandma's presence could be felt—never seen. She was more like Fiona's personal guardian angel—a caretaker to watch over her. Grandma was known to turn the porch light on when Fiona would arrive home later in the evening than expected. Grandma always had fresh coffee perking in the morning when she stumbled into the kitchen. Fiona kept the house so grandma could stay, and in turn, it seemed grandma looked after Fiona—it was a fine arrangement.

But…

Was she ready to share her grandma's ghostly presence with Nathan? Clearly, he'd become quite aware of grandma's activities in the house. Gram loved to play tricks on Nathan, like the lights going on and off or a candy dish moving about. Fiona had no trouble imagining her grandma's sheer delight in Nathan's baffled expressions and reactions. She truly believed it was Grandma Ev's way of letting her know she approved of Nathan.

Over the past two years, Fiona had been able to duck Nathan's inquiries about the strange goings-on in her house, but now, he was asking straight up. He was looking her square in the eye and asking if there was, in fact, a ghost in her house—and he was asking about the ghost by name.

How could she lie?

What would lying about Grandma Ev's presence say about their relationship?

She couldn't trust Nathan with the truth?

"Yes," she blurted out, then she blinked. Did she say that out loud? Had she just confessed that the spirit of Evelyn Burrell did, in fact, live in her house? Her eyes snapped to meet Nathan's, whose eyes were as big as saucers.

Appearing just as shocked by the answer as she was at giving it, he repeated, "*Yes*? Are you telling me your grandma's ghost lives in this house?"

There was no escape.

There was no taking it back.

The cat was out of the bag.

"Well, yes, I mean, kind of, she sort of…you know… she hangs out here. Not that I mind. She's perfectly welcome. Well, of course she is, she's my grandma. She's never a bother. Well, maybe to you she is, but now that you know she's here, it may not be so much of a bother.

She likes you, Nathan, I know she does. If Grandma didn't like you, she wouldn't play her little tricks on you. She's teasing you. Grandma Ev was always a tease—in a good way. Are you mad? You're not mad, are you? I know, I know, I should've told you long before this, but I just wasn't ready—especially when our relationship was new. I thought you'd think I was some kind of crazy, and I wouldn't have blamed you. Let's face it, you've met my family. And seriously, how many girlfriends have their grandmother's ghost living in their house? So, you're not mad, right?"

In silence, Nathan turned and wandered about the apartment. He looked at the old photographs on the end tables and on the tall dresser against the wall. With a svelte smile on his face, he reached down to give the old piano bench next to the dresser a spin. He'd been in the apartment several times before, but now that he knew about Grandma Ev's ghost, he seemed more interested or perhaps comfortable in the surroundings. Wincing, Fiona watched him make his way to the line of four short doors along the wall just at the top of the stairwell. The doors were only about four feet in height—storage space. He took hold of the small knob on the first door, then he hesitated to glance back at Fiona.

"She's not gonna jump out at me or anything if I open this, will she?" he inquired.

"No…no, of course not," Fiona assured.

"Good." He opened the door to peer inside, then he closed it. "Okay…so does she walk through the walls or sit on your bed and talk with you while you get ready for work in the morning?"

"No…it's nothing like that. Gram has never made an actual appearance, although I do believe Harriet can see her." Both Fiona and Nathan glanced over to where Harriet lay on Grandma's bed. The little Maltese was lying belly-up with her tiny pink tongue hanging out as if someone were scratching her tummy. Suddenly, the little Maltese's leg shivered madly. Shaking her head, Fiona turned to Nathan. "You didn't answer my question—are you mad?"

"No…I'm not mad. I knew something was going on in the house, just wasn't quite sure what or who. But this does not clarify, at all, that you're not some kind of crazy," Nathan said with a smirk on his lips. "That said, if you've never actually seen your grandmother's ghost, how do you know she's really here?"

Fiona let out a relieved breath. "Well, I can feel her, and she does little things to make her presence known." Around a chuckle, she added, "Like…turn the lights on and off with no warning. Or…make the staircase move like an escalator—"

His eyes widened with recollection. "Like when I first met you—the murder of that ballerina from the Benedum, Alexis Cartwright?"

"Uh, huh."

"So, she's a helpful ghost—kind of like Casper," Nathan put in.

"Um, not exactly, but you've got the idea."

Smiling his understanding, he lifted his face toward the ceiling as if Fiona's grandmother were dangling from the light fixture. "Hey, Evelyn, I'd like to formally introduce myself. I'm Nathan Landry, and I sure do adore your granddaughter—even if she is *all kinds* of crazy."

Just then, the lights in the attic went out.

Nathan sighed. "Yep, that's about right."

Fiona giggled.

Two

The glorious fall weather painted the trees with a brilliant gold and crimson pallet. The air was fresh and warm, yet a tiny hint of chill mixed in the breeze to remind western Pennsylvania that old man winter would soon be knocking at their door. Nonetheless, Fiona took advantage of the pleasant weather. She walked to and from the elementary school where she was a kindergarten teacher.

With house keys in hand and her backpack slung over her right shoulder, she made her way up the sidewalk toward the front porch of her house. As she pushed the front door open, she could hear Harriet fussing from inside her kennel. While holding the door open with her right foot, Fiona swept up the mail from the floor, then opened the kennel gate for Harriet to make her escape outside.

Waiting for her little Maltese to do her thing in the yard, then run back into the house, Fiona thumbed through two sales brochures from department stores, her water bill, the electric bill, and…she stilled at the sight of a yellowed envelope. Narrowing her eyes, she flipped the envelope over to see who the rumpled old envelope belonged to. Amazingly enough, the letter was addressed to Evelyn Burrell at 7 Guyland Street, Pittsburgh.

"Another one?" Fiona muttered to herself while pulling her foot from the door allowing it to drop closed. This time she'd received an envelope that appeared to be a letter rather than a greeting card. Again, the return address read, Lucille Smith, and again there was the official Dixmont postmark stationed near the postage stamp. Honestly, one of the most impressive parts about the mysterious mail was the price of the stamps affixed to the envelopes—*six cents*.

Setting aside her backpack and the less inspiring mail—the water and electric bills, she sat down on the bottom step to slip her finger along the flap of the envelope to see what Lucille had written in her letter to Gram. Perhaps the letter would shed some light on this enigmatic family member who no one wanted to talk about.

Why was Lucille in a mental facility?

Why did Gram have to take care of Lucille's son, Dick?

What happened to Lucille's husband?

More importantly, why was this mail arriving at her home on Oxford Street when the letters were specifically addressed to her grandmother at her former address on Guyland Street—almost two blocks away and several decades late?

Gingerly, Fiona eased the letter from the envelope and just as tentatively she opened the tri-folded paper. She took in a slight breath when her eyes fell upon Lucille's handwriting. Her cursive was rather large and slanted and dark as if she were pressing down very hard on the pencil. Fiona's heart sank—this was a message from one sister to another after years gone by. This was a note that had never been read, information never received, and possibly the absolute last correspondence from a woman desperate to be heard.

Or not.

Perhaps in the anticipation of reading the letter, she was creating more mellow-dramatic assumptions than the actual content would produce—perhaps.

Fiona took in another breath. She found herself trying to muster the courage to read the words Lucille had put to paper while in the confines of a state mental institution.

"You got one too?"

Fiona jumped almost dropping the letter to the floor. She looked up to see her eccentric neighbor, Astrid Dingle filling the doorway with a squirming Harriet under her arm. Now, there was someone who could use a little time in a mental institution, Fiona couldn't help but think. Astrid's long gray hair was pulled back into a braid, and much to Fiona's relief, she was wearing a pair of jean capris, a blouse, and a pair of dirty sneakers. Astrid fantasied herself as a clairvoyant of sorts. Oftentimes, she'd show up at the house dressed like a psychic or fortune teller. So far,

Grandma Ev wasn't terribly receptive, and Fiona was just as relieved with that.

"Astrid!" Fiona said with reprimand filling her tone. "What are you doing here? I've told you before, you shouldn't just walk into my house like that."

"Your dog was scratching on the door. You weren't letting her in. I think that might make you a bad pet parent," Astrid replied.

Straightening her spine, Fiona glowered at the woman. "Why would you care what kind of pet parent I am? You don't even like dogs."

Astrid set Harriet's paws to the floor, and the little dog rushed into Fiona's lap. "You're right. I don't. Anyway, it looks like you got some of that old mail that's being delivered around the neighborhood."

Fiona blinked back. "Other people in the neighborhood are receiving old mail?"

"Pat McCune from across the street has. She received a birthday card from her mom from 1971. How do ya like that?" Astrid let out a chuckle. "She said there was twenty bucks in it. What did you get?"

"Um…*I* didn't actually receive anything. A Christmas card for my Grandma Ev came yesterday, and today she received a letter from her sister—yesterday's postmark was dated, 1975, and this one is from 1976."

"Wow. Are you gonna read it?"

"After you leave."

"*Seriously*?"

"Seriously."

Around a loud *harrumph,* Astrid marched out of the house but turned back to pout at her through the screen door. "Will you at least let me know what's in the letter? Maybe I could speak with the spirit—"

Fiona leaned forward to push the front door closed. The moment Astrid would mention talking with spirits inside, outside, or anywhere near her house, that was the moment the conversation was done. Astrid had a tendency to whirl out of control when it came to spirits. If Fiona didn't nip Astrid's desire in the bud the whirling out of control would begin before she could put a stop to it. Astrid would show up with magic potions to fling in the air while muttering a weird mantra to supposedly draw spirits out.

No. Thank. You.

She could only hope that Pat McCune did not have a spirit in her house or that she had not agreed to allow Astrid inside to communicate with said spirit. Yikes. Setting Harriet on the step, she got up to lock the front door—no more interruptions from her kooky neighbor, Astrid.

Finally, alone with the letter, Fiona began to read…

Dear Evelyn,

I hope Dick is being a good boy. I know you are doing your best with him. I trust you. You are the sister who I trust. Alberta won't answer my letters. Anna has her own problems. I know you read my letters. I hope you will help me—even if it is only in your prayers.

Sincerely,
Lucille

Although the letter did not have a completely desperate tone to it, there was a hint of despair in who Lucille could trust—who she could count on to read her letters. If anyone was receiving said letters. What did Lucille want Gram to help her with? The subject was quite moot at this point—Gram never read Lucille's letter. Gram never knew what Lucille wanted her to do—unless there were other letters she had received. Fiona sincerely hoped so, and then it struck her—she knew someone who might just know a little something about Lucille. Mom.

She picked up her backpack from the floor to rummage through the front pocket looking for her cell phone. Scowling at her lack of commitment to clean out the pocket, she tossed several candy wrappers onto the decorative table near the stairs along with two pens, a sticky note with a phone number scribbled on it—who's number was that anyway? She had no recollection. A plastic cap from a water bottle—what the heck was that doing in there? A wrapper from a Snickers bar—Nathan must've shoved that in there just to torture her, well played. Finally, she came up with the cell phone.

As she pressed the button to dial up her mom, she glanced at the pile of debris she'd laid on the little table—yeah, she'd have to make a solid commitment to throw that stuff in the trash after she spoke to her mom. She should make the same commitment to go through the rest of her backpack to see what else was in there she could dispose of.

"Hello…" her mom began, pulling her from her muse.

"Hey, Mom, how are you doing today?"

"Fiona Nicole, are you aware that I haven't heard a word from you in a week?" She expelled a melancholy sigh. "Oh, well, I suppose I shouldn't complain. At least *you* call once every two weeks or so. Your brother—not so much. He's still alive, isn't he?"

Yep, her mother, Nancy Quinn, could be the master of guilt trips—the queen of manipulation.

Yeesh.

"I haven't heard anything different. I'm calling because I need some information," Fiona explained while she made her way to the living room. Plopping down onto the sofa, she lifted her legs onto the coffee table, crossing the right ankle over the left. Harriet immediately jumped up to curl up in her lap.

"Imagine my surprise. You're not calling just to chat—you need information," her mother whined.

"Come on now, Mom. I called you just last week and we had a lovely chat, remember? You told me all about the flower show you and dad attended in Daytona, and how nice it was that Aunt Diane and Uncle Mike came to visit, and what a beautiful young lady Madison was growing into."

Suddenly, her mom's voice brightened. "Oh, that's right. Okay, you're off the hook. Your brother—not so much. What information are you looking for?"

"Well, I was wondering about Great-Aunt Lucille—"

"Aunt *Lucille*? Good Lord in the morning, why would you ever wonder about her? She was mentally ill. She spent the latter part of her life in Dixmont and died there. Although she actually didn't spend too much time institutionalized—she died within a year, pneumonia, I think. That's about all I know about Aunt Lucille."

"Gram raised her son, Dick, didn't she? Where was her husband?" Fiona inquired.

"Yes, Dick lived with us until he graduated high school. You remember him—very good-looking, very charming. He was married about four times, I think. He finally married someone who could handle him." Around a snort, she added, "Someone who wasn't prettier than he was. Anyway, what's this sudden interest in Lucille Smith?"

Fiona went on to explain about the Christmas card and the letter she'd received on behalf of Grandma Ev.

Mom said, "Oh, my. Well, I don't know what to tell you, sweetie. Gram really never spoke of Lucille, and we never asked. Well, maybe Dick did but never in my presence. He may have asked her in private."

"Do you happen to know what happened to her husband?"

"No, not really. Dick had an older brother, Edward—that was Lucille's husband's name as well. And then there was a younger daughter, Blanche. They lived with different people—maybe Edward and Blanche lived with the father's family. I really can't say. I never saw them or met them, and no one really knew what happened to Lucille's husband. He was just—*gone*, it seemed."

"I wonder if I'll receive any more letters or if this is the end of it all. I sure am intrigued," Fiona said.

Her mother's sigh wafted through the connection. "Well, I'm sure they're all dead by now. Dick was quite older than I was—by fifteen years, and I heard he passed about a year or so ago. Edward is gone as well. I don't know a thing about Blanche. I'm surprised I remembered her name for that matter. So, I guess my question is, where are these letters coming from? Did the post office just come across them or did the dead letter office finally figure out where they were supposed to go?"

"I don't know. I heard that some of the other neighbors are receiving old mail too. I'm going to make an effort to see the mailman and question him about the letters."

"Good idea. Do you know who the new mailman is? I heard old Mr. Bixby finally retired—it was about time. I swear he'd delivered the mail since about 1918."

Fiona chuckled. "He was pretty old. But in his defense, as old as he was, he walked his route every day since…well…like you said, about 1918."

Mom returned Fiona's chortle. "Agreed. That said, if you want to know more about Lucille…you know where to find Gram."

Moments after Fiona disconnected her call with her mom she found herself in the foyer looking up the staircase. She'd never tried to communicate with Grandma Ev—never once. Yes, she could feel her presence in the household. She knew when she was nearby, but other than make little comments into thin air directed at her late grandmother, Fiona had never tried to actually seek her out.

Was now the time?

Would Grandma Ev communicate with her?

What would that look like?

She glanced down at the letter in her hand and had to wonder if this had been the one and only correspondence Lucille had sent to Gram. If Gram did not respond, perhaps Lucille did not make another attempt—after all, Lucille mentioned in the letter that Alberta had not answered her letters.

Was it possible that Alberta had not received her letters either?

If the neighbors were receiving long-lost mail, as she was, perhaps there was an entire lot of mail from the same time period that had been misplaced or lost or—who knew?

A wave of pity washed through Fiona's gut. This poor woman may have been reaching out to her sisters for help and understanding only to have the US mail completely fail her. How awful.

For Lucille's sake, Fiona needed to climb the stairs into the attic and at least try to communicate with Grandma Ev. Hey, there was a first time for everything and maybe, just maybe, Grandma Ev would be receptive to this one-time conversation.

With renewed purpose, Fiona eased the letter back into the envelope, her cell phone into her hip pocket, then climbed the staircase. Harriet scurried past her to beat her to the second floor. The little Maltese pranced alongside her ankles as she made her way to the door that led to the third-floor apartment.

This was it.

Fiona climbed the stairs and flicked on the lights. She stood at the apex of the stairs, looking into the living space her grandmother had once occupied. The room was hot, as it always was during the warm-weather months. With measured steps, she went to the sofa covered with a white sheet and pulled it aside to carefully drape it over the right-half of the green chenille couch, then she eased down, and Harriet sat beside her.

She was truly amazed at how comfortable she actually felt. She'd sat on this couch with Grandma Ev on many a Sunday afternoon watching old movies while sipping tea. This was the couch she sat upon the first time she saw *Gone with the Wind*. She remembered being awestruck by Shirley Jones in the musical, *Oklahoma*, and she could never forget the fabulous, Natalie Wood in *West Side Story*. Grandma loved those old films, and Fiona found that she loved them too.

This was the couch where she'd had many a conversation with her grandmother, and she closed her eyes to try as hard as she might to remember any conversation she may have had about Lucille. Fiona sat very still, taking her time, using the meditation techniques she'd been taught in yoga class. Listening to her breath flowing in and then going out, she blocked out all the sounds around her—the sound of cars traveling up Oxford Street, of Harriet moving about to make herself comfy on the couch, and then the memory came to her...

She could see Grandma dusting her apartment one afternoon when she came up the stairs. Grandma turned and smiled at her. She remembered that Grandma had removed a plant from what looked like a small bench next to her dresser, and she was wiping the top of the bench down.

Fiona asked, "What's that?"

Grandma stilled. She seemed to be studying the bench, and Fiona recalled she had a rather sad look on her face. "That," Grandma began. "Is an old piano bench—it belonged to my sister, Lucille. Oh, how she could play the piano, and she never had a lesson—our parents could've never afforded anything like that. Piano lessons were too dear. But Lucille had a natural talent and taught herself how to play. Now it's just a place for me to put this silly plant." She set the long-vined plant back in its place.

"Where's Lucille now?" Fiona asked.

"Oh, she's been gone for quite some time now—over twenty years. My how time flies," grandma replied as she made her way toward the coffee table to continue her dusting.

"What happened to her?"

"Oh, Lucille had some problems. She couldn't handle what life threw at her. She ended up in a mental hospital and never came out. It was a shame."

Fiona had pressed Gram for yet more information. "Why did she go to the mental hospital?"

Grandma shrugged. "She just couldn't handle certain things—like, um, she had some trouble with her husband, and she…well, she just couldn't handle it is all. Hey, Singing in the Rain will be on later. Want to watch it with me? I bought a bag of Doritos—I know they're your favorite."

But Fiona couldn't be swayed from her inquiry about

grandma's mysterious sister. "What happened to Lucille's husband? Did he leave her for another woman?"

Again, grandma stilled. "I'm not sure, Fiona. We'll never know what ever became of Edward."

Fiona opened her eyes. Yes, she remembered that conversation with her grandmother. Now she was even more fascinated by Lucille's situation and what happened to her husband, Edward. She pushed up from the couch and made her way to the desk near the window, opened the center drawer where her grandmother had kept Christmas cards and added Lucille's letter to the pile.

"In case you want to read it, Gram," she whispered.

Her cell phone rang causing her to flinch. Pulling the cell from her pocket, she looked at the screen: Nathan Landry.

"Hello…"

"Hey, Fiona, I think I need your help—right away," Nathan said.

He sounded a bit stressed. Trying to remain calm, Fiona asked, "What's wrong? Where are you?"

"Presbyterian Hospital."

"Oh, my God, Nathan, are you all right?"

"Yeah, I am—Tavia's not."

THREE

Fiona's heart was in her throat. "What's going on? What happened? Is Tavia going to be okay?"

Around a beleaguered sigh, Nathan replied, "Yeah, she'll be okay in about *four* weeks." He let out another careworn breath. "She broke her ankle, or should I say, *I* broke her ankle."

"Okay…I'm almost afraid to ask, but…how did *you* break Tavia's ankle?"

A long silence followed. It was most obvious by the shuffling of the phone on the other end that Fiona could detect Nathan was searching for the words to confess…something, and she had a feeling what that something just might be.

"Um…well…I kinda stepped on her foot while I was trying to help her turn while we were changing positions, and…well…she twisted her ankle completely around and fell. When I say she twisted her ankle completely around…I mean in a 360-degree twist. That baby snapped like a twig. It made a really loud—"

"I get the idea, Nathan! So, I'm taking it that you were at your ballroom lesson when this occurred?"

"Yep. Let's just say we won't be attending any more classes with Ms. Angela—even if Tavia could. Before I got in the ambulance with Tav, Ms. Angela told me to never step foot in the studio again." Nathan's voice was filled with gloom.

Oh, dear.

Poor Nathan.

Fiona couldn't help herself. She had to ask, "There was an *ambulance* involved?"

Another burdened sigh. "Yeah. We were afraid to move her—a bone was—"

"Never mind! I *don't* want to know!"

"Well, *you* asked," he pointed out.

"And I'm sorry I did. So, now what?"

"Well…that's what we need to talk about. Right after I talk to my captain."

"What do you mean?"

"I still have an investigation to complete, and now I need a dance partner. Don't say anything…just listen. You have plenty of dance experience, being that you were almost a ballerina. So, I figure with your grace and knowledge of dance, you might be able to pull me through this mess."

"I studied *ballet*, Nathan, not ballroom dancing. Those are two *completely* different styles of dance. I don't know the first thing about ballroom dancing."

"I hear ya, Fiona. And we don't have an instructor either, but I've got to come up with a partner and an instructor right quick or this investigation will go sideways. Now, are ya with me?"

She could hear the pleading in his voice.

He was desperate.

How could she say no?

Letting out her own haggard sigh, Fiona replied, "Okay, I'm in. But I think we should visit Tavia to see how she's doing, and then I'm going to talk to a friend of mine who used to do some ballroom to see if she might help us. And you're on notice, Detective—I'd better not break any bones."

"Silja?" Nathan asked.

"You got it," Fiona said.

Nathan's voice instantly sounded elated, or perhaps, relieved. "Thanks, Fiona. You're a peach!" With that, he cut off the connection—probably so she didn't have time to recant.

Fiona pressed the *end* button on her cell, then thumbed through her *favorites* to find an old friend who she felt sure she could count on—Silja (Sil-ya) Ramsay. She and Silja had studied ballet together at Pittsburgh Ballet Theater as teens—Silja went on to become a professional ballerina, but due to a severe knee injury, Fiona decided to become a teacher. She remembered that along with studying to become a ballerina, Silja did a little competing in the ballroom dancing circles when she was in her late teens and early twenties.

This was a huge favor to ask.

This was a huge undertaking for herself and for Silja.

Was she insane to agree to this debacle?

Looking down at the letter from her great-aunt Lucille lying in the desk drawer, she muttered, "Maybe *I* should check into a facility—if there are any nowadays." With that, she eased the desk drawer closed to make her way downstairs while trying to muster the courage to call Silja and ask for that really big favor.

∽ ∽ ∽

"You really are somethin', Landry. First, you break one of our most game officer's ankle, and now, you're not even a little afraid to ask your girl to take on the risk of becoming your dance partner. What are you, some kind of sadist?"

Detective Nathan Landry fell back against the chair he sat on. "I didn't break Tavia's ankle on purpose, and no, I am not into hurting other people, but I've got to get this case off the ground. That said, I think the only way to do that is to have a dance partner who isn't trying to learn how to dance—just leading me along. I think Fiona can do that. Hey, she did a great job several years ago when we asked her to go undercover as a ballerina during the Alexa Cartwright murder investigation. Not to mention, she did a great job when we asked her to pretend like she'd won the lottery during the Lucky Maguire murder investigation not too long ago."

"Tell me again…why does this girl want to be involved with you?"

The detective's lips curled into a sly smirk. "Because not only am I dashingly good-looking, but I'm also charming and suave."

The captain pointed his finger at Detective Landry. "Listen, Mr. Good-looking, charming, and suave, you make sure Ms. Quinn comes out of this unharmed or I'll break more than your ankle. You hear me?"

"Loud and clear, Cap'n, loud and clear."

The captain plopped back against his seat folding his hands over his belly. "Okay, so, where are we on the case?"

Detective Landry opened the old yellowed file lying in his lap. "Our suspect from more than forty years ago is a Mr. Vincent Di Volante. At the time of the murders, Mr. Di Volante was twenty-eight years of age and pretty well-known as a ballroom dancer. We have three male victims of various ages, Anthony Martinez, twenty-five, Harris Bradley, twenty-nine, and…Blake Dennison, thirty-two. The common denominator seems to be a ballroom dancer by the name of, Isadora Danza—still living. Both she and Di Volante were children of Italian immigrants—hm, I find it interesting that information is mentioned in the report. Anyway, at the time of the murders, Ms. Danza was twenty-six, so that would make her about… sixty-nine or so."

The captain inquired, "Love triangle?"

"From the interview notes, I don't think so. I think it was more about eliminating the competition. At the time, Ms. Danza was hot on the ballroom circuit—unbeatable. And quite beautiful, too." He plucked a photograph of a gorgeous woman dressed in a red sequin ballroom gown from the file and tossed it across the desk to the captain.

The captain picked up the photo. His eyebrows rose in admiration. "Yes, she certainly was, and maybe she still is." He lifted another photo from the file. "I see we have an old photo of Di Volante too—really old. Was this Di Volante getting rid of dancers so he could be her partner or was he a jealous lover?"

"That's the only picture I've been able to locate of Di Volante—which is really weird. Anyway, in the interviews, Ms. Danza claimed she had no relationship with Di Volante. She claimed he was a mediocre dancer, and she wasn't interested in him as a partner or in any other way. She said he was constantly showering her with flowers and gifts, including jewelry the dancers wear during competition, to try to win her over."

"No luck?"

"Evidently not. So, I guess Di Volante decided to pick off his competition one by one. Anyway, the lead investigator on the case…" The detective flipped back to the front page, "Detective Jake Rowan, broke the case. I guess he and some of the guys had Di Volante trapped inside a house one night, only Di Volante managed to give them the slip. Rowan caught sight of him getting into a vehicle parked along the street and they pursued him at high speeds. That's when things got hairy. Di Volante, or at least they *assumed* it was Di Volante, flipped the car and it burst into flames. The driver was burned beyond recognition. Di Volante never surfaced again, until recently," the detective explained.

"Talk to Rowan…see what he remembers about the case," the captain instructed.

"Can't. He retired from the force ten years ago and died of cancer three years ago," Detective Landry said. "But, we do have a retired detective who was on the case…Norm Yallowitz."

"Whoa. He would've been a young detective back then. Wonder if he had narcolepsy back in the day."

"Don't know. Anyway, I'm gonna drop by his place tomorrow to see how he remembers it. As you know, Di Volante's fingerprints were found at the home of a recently deceased, Angelo Moretti. Turns out, Mr. Moretti is Isadora Danza's brother. Her fingerprints were not found at his home, but that may mean she's simply never been fingerprinted."

"Seems to be a theme here," the captain interjected.

"Yeah, well, it looks like we buried our murderer over forty years ago, but my gut is telling me the person in his grave isn't Di Volante. So, we may have a fourth victim. We need to find out who's in that grave. I've got a request in to exhume Di Volante's body. So far, the girl at Tavia's desk—what's her name again?"

"Amanda."

"Yeah, that's right, Amanda. Anyway, Amanda has not come up with any living relatives for Mr. Di Volante, so it's looking good to get that clearance on exhuming the body right quick."

"Okay then, get to it, Landry. And while you're at it, see if you can track down Ms. Danza. Make absolutely sure she hasn't seen or heard from Di Volante since his *alleged* death."

"I'm all over it—right after Fiona and I visit Tavia in the hospital."

The captain fell back against his seat. "For your sake, I hope she's not armed."

❧ ❧ ❧

Fiona wasn't sure if she should feel happy or horrified. Silja's husband, Grant was out of town. Silja's dance school hadn't reopened from the summer break just yet, so she merrily agreed to travel from Harverton, Pennsylvania to Pittsburgh and stay at Fiona's home, while giving her and Nathan ballroom dancing instruction.

Even though Fiona had explained Nathan's lack of grace, Silja had no idea what she'd gotten herself into.

Yikes.

Meanwhile, a to-do list was piling up inside Fiona's head—Silja would arrive tomorrow afternoon. Snacks— she needed snacks. And wine—Silja liked a nice dry red, usually a pinot. There was a bit of housework to do as well—she should strip the bed in the guest room and provide fresh sheets for her visitor or hostage as it may very well turn out.

Double yikes.

She groaned. It was becoming more and more apparent that sitting on the couch watching TV would not be an option this evening. Unfortunately, a trip to the basement to visit the washing machine, then a trip to the grocery was in order; furthermore, the guest room wasn't going to clean itself.

❧ ❧ ❧

Tavia sat up from the pillow in her hospital bed. "*Seriously*, Fiona? After what *I've* been through, after what *you've* witnessed with your own two eyes, you're gonna take dance class with this…this…*galoot*. I can't believe it! He's dangerous. He's a disaster in dance shoes."

Letting out a sigh, Fiona glanced at Nathan who was leaning against the wall looking most dejected. "I get it. I do. But someone's gotta do this, and it looks like that someone is me. C'mon, it makes perfect sense. I've danced all my life—not ballroom, mind you, but dance is dance. I think if anyone can help him through this and survive—it's me."

Nathan made his way to the foot of the bed. "I'm really sorry, Tav. Can ya forgive me?" Letting out a groan, she fell back against the pillow. He pulled a box from behind his back. "I brought ya a big box of salted chocolate caramels. The kind you really, really like from Yetta's Candy."

Tavia tossed him a look.

He stretched the box out toward her. "Did I mention they're *salted* caramels?"

She turned toward him with tight lips.

"From *Yetta's* Candy, on *Grant* Avenue—"

She snatched the box from his hand. "Okay, okay, you're forgiven. Now get outta here so I can binge in private."

Smiling, Nathan turned to Fiona who was waving him toward the door in a rushed fashion.

Just before Nathan stepped into the hallway, Tavia called after him. "Hey, Landry! Don't hurt the kindergarten teacher or I'll hunt you down!"

With his hands on Fiona's lower back, Nathan urged her to move quickly down the hall. "Man, I'd hate to see what she'd say if she hadn't forgiven me."

"Good thing you brought the chocolate," Fiona added.

FOUR

Fiona hurried home from school. She felt lucky to have gotten half the day off so early in the school year. She wanted to be present when Silja arrived and hoped she'd bump into her mailman. Perhaps he could shed some light on why the letters from so long ago were finally showing up—at least, she hoped he could. After parking her Mini Cooper on the street in front of her house, she rushed up the sidewalk, and as per usual, she could hear Harriet barking from her kennel. She unlocked and opened her front door only to find the mail had already arrived.

Harriet barked her impatience through the gate of her kennel, while Fiona scooped up the small amount of mail she'd received—a bank statement and a pamphlet announcing the fall schedule for Pittsburgh Ballet Theater's performances at the Benedum Center, downtown.

Nothing from Lucille.

Ignoring Harriet's demands for freedom, Fiona scanned the foyer floor to make sure she hadn't missed a card or an envelope lying about.

Nothing—well, except for that sticky-note with the unidentified phone number scribbled on it. She dragged her gaze toward the decorative table that still held the stuff she'd cleaned out of her backpack the day before. She sighed. How could she have missed that stuff when she was cleaning up last night? She grabbed the note from the floor and the assortment of garbage she'd left on the decorative table to throw in the trash.

She was a bit taken aback by her own disappointment that there had been no long-lost letter from years ago delivered. So, was that it? Was the letter she'd received yesterday from Lucille the last correspondence from Grandma's sister? If so, what happened? Did Lucille ever see her children or her husband again, or did she die with no further communication? What a dreadful thought.

Harriet's protest hitched up an octave, jerking Fiona from her funk. "Sorry, baby, I'm a little preoccupied." She opened the gate to let the little dog make a mad dash down the hall into the kitchen, through the dining room, across the living room, leap onto the couch, dive off of the couch, and back into the foyer where she held the door open. The little white flash of lightning rushed out to the yard. Leaving the front door open while letting the screen drop closed, Fiona made her way into the kitchen to dispose of the small pile of trash. With narrowed eyes, she examined the telephone number on the sticky note trying to remember whose number it was and why she had kept it. With nothing coming to mind, she discarded the note with the other trash, and that's when she smelled the welcoming aroma of freshly brewed coffee. Glancing across the counter, she noticed the full pot of coffee in the coffeemaker. The coffeemaker let out a loud *pop* as if to announce, *coffee's ready*!

Fiona had to smile, Grandma Ev must've felt she needed some comfort coffee, or she was trying to tell her something.

"I see your grandma has made us a fresh pot. We can always count on, Grandma Evie, to fulfill our every coffee desire." Silja's voice took Fiona by surprise.

She whirled around to find the tall, lean, lovely brunette filling the doorway with Harriet tucked under her right arm and a smile on her pretty face. Fiona found it most adorable that Silja had come up with her own endearment for Grandma Ev. "You remembered."

Silja let out a snort. "How could I forget? How many girls have their grandma's ghost living in their attic, and how many of those ghosts make coffee on the spot, can you tell me that?" Silja plopped a kiss on Fiona's cheek, and in an exaggerated sexy voice, she asked, "So, how've ya been, Sugar Twin?"

Fiona giggled at her old friend's silly antics. "Oh, Silja, you never change—thank God for that. I've got so much to tell you. Good thing Grandma's on top of her game."

"You can say that again." She looked up to the ceiling and saluted. "Thanks, Grandma Evie—you're the ghostess with the mostest. By the way, I found this in your front yard," Silja nodded toward Harriet, then placed the bundle of fluff into Fiona's arms. "I think that might make you a bad pet parent."

Fiona rolled her eyes as she set Harriet's paws to the floor. "She was doing her thing. You have a pet, don't you?"

"I have a cat."

"Mm, that's more like having a boss than a pet."

"Tell me about it. Okay, girlfriend, pour the Joe. I want to hear all about this ballroom dancing gig the three of us are going on, your romance with the cutie-pie detective, and anything else you want to confess."

Fiona chuckled. "This could take all afternoon."

"Perfect. I just happen to be available."

ξ∂ ξ∂ ξ∂

The caretaker at Jefferson Memorial Cemetery, located within the South Hills area of Pittsburgh, stood next to Detective Landry while examining a grave. "Won't take me long to open the grave, Detective."

"Thanks. Hey, I noticed the sign as I came in that says the cemetery has camera surveillance at all times."

"Sure do. With so many cemeteries getting vandalized nowadays—ya gotta do what ya gotta do. It's a sad state of affairs, that's for sure."

"I hear ya. How long do yinz keep the footage?" Detective Landry inquired.

"Don't know for sure, but at least thirty days. We helped the police with a murder that took place right here in the cemetery a couple years back. Ever since then, we keep them for a good month, I think—costs the cemetery a pretty penny too. The images are loaded onto one of those clouds, that way we don't have to fuss with the chip—I know that much." The caretaker climbed up on the backhoe.

Detective Landry glanced down to find a single withered and rumpled rose lying at the base of the headstone. He bent down and cautiously lifted the rose; many of the browned curled petals fell away leaving only one or two clinging to the stem. Carefully, he pushed the pitiful rose into the left pocket of his jacket. He would need to place it into an evidence bag the moment he returned to his SUV. "Hey, do ya think you could get me the last thirty days of video?"

"No problem. I can have the office send it in an email."

"Ah, if ya don't mind, I'd prefer a DVD—just in case I need it for evidence at a later date."

"No problem, I'll have them send that over, and I'll have this grave open in a jiffy," the caretaker yelled down from his seat on the backhoe.

Detective Landry nodded in reply, pulled a bite-size Snickers bar from his right pocket, then began to unwrap the candy. The detective moved back to stand near a tall black granite headstone. While keeping a close eye on the backhoe digging up a grave marked, *Vincent Di Volante, February 3, 1946-April 2, 1976,* he tossed the bite-size candy into his mouth.

The detective was glad it was a nice sunny day—exhuming a body from its resting place was unpleasant business when the sun was shining, it was really nasty in the rain, wind, and mud. He hated disturbing the deceased, except he was almost certain Vincent Di Volante was not occupying that grave. Who was? He had no idea. He was most hopeful the coroner would be able to identify the remains through DNA testing.

"Why are you digging up that grave?" a woman's voice with a slight Italian accent yelled above the choke and grind of the backhoe's engine. Her voice came from behind the gravestone the detective had almost leaned against.

He jumped and then turned to find an older well-dressed woman who was wearing a floral scarf wrapped around her head, a pair of rhinestone-studded sunglasses, and a gold pantsuit. The woman was thin and through the scarf, he could see she had dark hair. The detective yelled over the roar of the backhoe's efforts, "I'm sorry, I hope we weren't disturbing you."

Pulling the scarf closer to her neck, she said, "My parents and my brother are buried across the way. I came to place flowers on their graves and saw you disturbing this grave. Is the family moving him?"

Closing the distance between them so he could hear her better, he said, "No, ma'am. I'm Detective Nathan Landry, Pittsburgh Homicide Unit. Did you know Mr. Di Volante?" He dug into the right pocket of his jacket to pull out several of the small Snickers bars.

She shot a quick glance over her shoulder at a silver sedan with dark tinted windows parked on the driveway in the distance. She said, "We were…acquainted."

He held out the tiny chocolate bars to the woman. "Snickers? They're bite-size. Perfect for a little pick-me-up. If you need one."

Her pink-glossed lips curled, and to his surprise, she took one of the candies from his palm and dropped it into her handbag. "For later."

He unwrapped one of the Snickers. Even though the older woman was sporting sunglasses, she was lovely, and he had a hunch. "You look very familiar." He tossed the chocolate candy into his mouth while shaking his finger at her. "I know I've seen you somewhere before. Do you do commercials on TV?"

The woman snorted. "For wrinkle cream?"

Around a chuckle, he replied, "I don't see any wrinkles. You know, I've been watching a lot of internet videos lately. My girl and I are doing a little ballroom dancing—is that where I've seen you?"

The woman drew her hand to her chest while tossing him a demure smile. "I'm flattered. Yes, I've done my fair share of videos. Are you enjoying it?"

"Enjoying what?"

"The ballroom dancing—are you enjoying it?"

"Um…yeah, I guess so."

"Oh, no, you must be passionate about the dance—you must dance it with your *soul*," the woman insisted.

"I knew it—you have to be the one and only, Isadora Danza," the detective exclaimed.

Smiling, the woman glanced at the sedan, then touched his arm. "You may call me Izzy—Isadora is an old woman's name."

Just then the backhoe's engine coughed then silenced. The caretaker yelled, "The grave's open, Detective. Lemme put the backhoe away and get the hoist to open the crypt, then we'll lift the coffin, then I'll make the arrangements for that video to be sent to your precinct. Where's the coroner's van?"

Detective Landry turned to see the driver's window in the sedan was partially down, and the coroner's van just pulling through the cemetery's entrance in the distance. "They're here now." With that, the caretaker restarted the backhoe to make his way slowly across the graveyard.

"If you will excuse me, Detective. I don't care to witness this, but it was very nice to meet you," Izzy said as she turned to hurry away.

The detective took several strides toward the grave, craned his neck to look down into the hole, then turned to call after her, "Ms. Danza…" She turned. "Mr. Di Volante was a ballroom dancer too—is that how you were acquainted with him?"

"I…I believe you may be right, Detective. Thank you for the candy bar, take care." She quickened toward the sedan. The driver's side window closed as she approached the vehicle.

FIVE

Fiona flicked on the basement lights. She and Silja descended the old wooden stairs with Harriet on their heels. "It's not pretty, like I'm sure your dance studio is, and it's rather dank, but it's a large open space—big enough for us to move around and practice," Fiona explained, as they stepped away from the stairs into the basement area. She made her way toward a wood rack that was stationed next to the dryer.

"I'm impressed. It's wide open. Most basements have all kinds of junk piled in them—this is completely clear. Kudos to you, Quinn," Silja remarked.

As she gathered several pairs of panties and bras that had been air drying on the rack, Fiona said over her shoulder, "Well, it wasn't always like this. We filled two of those dumpster things before Mom and Dad moved to Florida three years ago. I guess I haven't had time to fill the place up, and I hope I never do. I like it like this. You brought music, I hope. I have an old CD player upstairs that I can bring down—we can set it on top of the dryer.

Or I can bring the TV stand down from grandma's apartment." She tucked the freshly folded undergarments under some brightly colored folded towels in a laundry basket atop the dryer.

Silja waved a careless hand. "I'm sure Grandma Evie wouldn't mind, but we won't need it. I downloaded a bunch of appropriate music on my tablet—we're good to go. So, when's twinkle toes arriving?"

"He's here now," Nathan said from the staircase. The girls turned. In his right hand he held a bouquet of red roses and in the other a bunch of roses that were peach in color.

Fiona leaned in close to Silja and whispered, "Okay, I'm figuring the red roses are for me because they are the color of romance, but you're the expert on this, what does the other color signify?"

Silja whispered back, "Your detective knows his roses—peach is the color of gratitude or appreciation."

Fiona snorted. "He outta be grateful for what he's about to put you through."

Silja snorted right back, "*I'm* not dancing with him, love."

With a bright smile on his face, Nathan made his way to the girls. Giving Fiona the red roses, he kissed her lips, and presenting Silja with the peach roses, he kissed her cheek. "I really appreciate you coming all this way to help us out, Silja, thanks."

"I was happy to do it," Silja said. "These are lovely, thank you."

"How long did you dance in the ballroom competitions?" Nathan inquired.

"Mm, about four years, I suppose. I wasn't full-time. I had my ballet classes and career to consider. I did it for fun, and it was, until I was done," Silja explained.

"Do you know a dancer named, Isadora Danza?"

"*Thee* Isadora Danza? Anybody who's anybody in the world of ballroom dancing knows who Isadora Danza is. She was world-class. She's fairly old now, but I believe she's still active—she judges, and I heard she travels the world to teach master classes—spends a lot of time out of the country too."

"So, you know her personally?" Nathan asked.

"No, I've never had the pleasure, but I've read many articles and interviews with her in my dance magazines," Silja explained.

"My research has turned up quite a few videos on the internet featuring her when she was a young dancer," Nathan said as he pulled his cell phone from his hip pocket and poked at the buttons. "And, I've found several more recent videos of her dancing with an older gentleman." He held the phone out for Silja and Fiona to watch a video he'd pulled up. The girls huddled around to view the video. "Do you know who the man is she's dancing with?"

Silja continued to study the video with narrowed eyes. "No...actually, the way the video is shot, you can't see his face." She watched a bit longer, then added, "Ever—they *never* show his face."

Nathan clicked on to another video. "I found this one from about seven months ago..."

Again, Fiona and Silja gathered around to view the film clip on Nathan's phone. Fiona said, "It's obviously the same man in this video as the last—you can tell by his hair, his posture, and his style of movement, but again, they never show you his face."

"Maybe because this video is all about Isadora—and he is secondary, a prop, if you will," Silja supplied.

"Still, how strange is it that there are no angles where you can see his face?" Fiona put in.

"Isadora Danza's not a suspect in your investigation, is she?" Silja asked.

"Hope not." Turning the phone off, he shoved it back into his pocket. "Are we gonna start where Tavia and I left off—the mambo?"

"Wow. The instructor started you off with the mambo? I would've started with something simpler, like the waltz," Silja said.

"Sounds *boring*," Nathan said.

"Sounds *safer*," Fiona said.

"Sounds like I should go upstairs to get the music and let the two of you sort this out in private. I'll bring down a couple of vases, and we'll keep the roses down here—it'll brighten the place up a bit," Silja suggested.

"You'll find vases under the kitchen sink. I think we should warm up with the waltz, and if I don't have any major bruising, we'll move on to the mambo," Fiona called after her. Turning to Nathan, she asked, "Fair enough?"

He reached into his pocket to pull out a small Snickers bar. "Compromise—that's what relationships are all about, compromise, right?"

"Smart man, that detective of yours," Silja noted, as she climbed the stairs.

It was three hours later when Fiona dropped onto the couch. "Ugh! Honestly, I adore that man, but I don't think I've ever been so happy to see him go home as I was tonight." Around a groan, she pulled off her shoes to rub her feet.

Dragging her fingers through the band that held her hair in a ponytail to let it spill about her shoulders, Silja plopped into the stuffed chair nearby. "Oh, I dunno, I didn't think he did all that badly. He caught on to the waltz rather quickly, and he didn't knock you to the floor, kick you in the shins, or break any of your bones when we worked on the mambo moves. He only stepped on your feet once or twice—not bad, considering the terrifying reports I got about his former classes. He tries really hard. I'm thinking we can move it all up a notch tomorrow night. After all, we really don't have that much time."

"You're right. I shouldn't complain—no ambulance had to be called, but my feet are killing me."

"By the way," Silja began. "I brought along my old ballroom dresses for you to try. When is the big event and where is it being held?"

"I think we have about a week, and the competition is taking place at the David L. Lawrence Convention Center, downtown."

Silja sat straight up in her seat. "The *Convention Center*? Surely, you're not competing in the *Glass Sipper*? I thought you were talking about a small competition—a local thing. The Glass Slipper is huge—Isadora Danza huge. She's probably one of the judges. You're not going to be able to fake your way through that. The dancers will come in from everywhere and they'll be fantastic."

Fiona's chest tightened. "Well...um...I'm sure we'll be in the novice division. I'm sure Nathan doesn't expect to win...or place...we're just there to...it's part of his investigation—"

"I'm not sure how. You'll be eliminated in the first round."

"Of the *novice* division?

Silja tossed her hands in the air. "Those novices have been practicing for *months*. You might've gotten through the first round if you were dancing with a more experienced partner, but with Nathan—I don't think so."

"I thought you said we were doing well and you wanted to move things up a notch tomorrow."

"I did, and you are, but not *Glass Sipper* well," Silja supplied.

Fiona lifted a shoulder. "I'm sure he has a plan—Nathan always does. We'll just keep plowing forward and whatever happens...happens."

"Oh, I know *exactly* what's going to happen."

Yikes—no, *double* yikes.

SIX

"Norm!" Detective Landry yelled as he pounded on the door of a small red-brick house with red and white striped metal awnings covering the windows and the small stoop at the front door. Retired, Detective Norman Yallowitz lived in the Dormont neighborhood of Pittsburgh. His aged sedan was parked in the driveway, so Landry figured he should be at home. However, the old detective suffered from narcolepsy, and when he was in the throes of a narcoleptic episode, he tended to be difficult to stir. Detective Landry pounded on the door again. "Norm! It's me, Nate Landry, open up!"

Finally, the door flung open. Detective Landry flinched turning his head away while squeezing his eyes closed. "Good God, Norm! Why would ya come to the door like that?"

"Because you were poundin' on my door like my place was on fire, that's why," the old detective groused. He was wearing a damp dingy green striped towel wrapped around his waist and a shower cap upon his mostly bald head. Soapy lather dripped from his shoulders and over his big belly, while he clutched a sudsy loofa sponge on a stick in his left hand. "Now, what do ya want? I'm tryin' to shower here."

Detective Landry waved his arms at Yallowitz to shoo him inside the house. "Well, get inside! I don't want anyone to see us, rather, *you,* like this."

Norm backed up giving Landry entry into the tiny unkempt living room. Leaning out of the door, he looked right then left and after closing the door, he snarled, "What are ya doing here, and you'd better not have that *woman* with ya."

"What woman?"

"Your girl's mother. What's her name again? Nancy— Nancy Quinn. She ain't nothin' but trouble."

Detective Landry shook his head. "You can say that again. No, she's not here."

"Well, thank sweet Jesus for that. Now, what's this about?" Yallowitz asked.

"Vincent Di Volante, do you remember him? He was a ballroom dancer."

Wiping the suds from his neck then swiping them onto the towel around his tubby waist, Yallowitz replied, "Yeah, I remember that case—not too often do ya investigate ballroom dancers. That was a long time ago, Landry. I was a young detective back then."

"You sure were—just getting started."

"Di Volante's dead. Why are you askin' about him?"

"I just had his body exhumed, or at least I had *somebody's* body exhumed. Wyatt Hays was called to a robbery in Upper St. Clair. Believe it or not, they dusted the house for prints. Di Volante, who is *supposed* to be dead, left prints all over the living room."

Yallowitz blinked back. "No way. Di Volante burned to death in his car. It flipped over. We chased him for… man, I don't remember how many blocks. What did the homeowner have to say?"

"Couldn't question the homeowner, he's deceased, but the daughter had no idea who Di Volante could be," Detective Landry explained. "Now, here's an interesting little tidbit. The homeowner was an Angelo Moretti— Isadora Danza's brother."

"Again, *long* time ago, but that name sounds familiar," Yallowitz said.

"I thought Di Volante was killing ballroom dancers who were partnered with Isadora, and I thought it stated in her interviews that she wanted no part of Di Volante," Detective Landry said.

"Your point?"

"That's what I was worried about. Okay, time to visit Izzy Danza," Landry said, as he turned for the door.

"Hold on! Lemme get some clothes on. I'm comin' with ya's," Yallowitz exclaimed.

"You're retired," Landry pointed out.

"She was one gorgeous woman. I wanna see what she looks like now. But don't get no grand ideas that I'm helpin' with the case. I'm *done* with that stuff." Yallowitz spun on his heels to hurry away when his towel let go, falling to the floor.

Detective Landry winced, covering his eyes. "Aw, Norm! I'm never gonna be able to un-see that!"

❧ ❧ ❧

Fiona hated leaving Silja home alone all day, but she had to be in her fresh kindergarten class for the new school year. Silja mentioned she'd be making a trip to the Robinson Mall in Robinson township—it was one of Sil's favorite shopping haunts when she visited Pittsburgh. She also mentioned she might stop in at the Benedum to visit some of her former ballet friends—they were rehearsing for one of the fall productions. Fiona was relieved Silja had places to go and people to see to keep her busy while she was at school.

The day before, Fiona was thrilled about Silja's visit, but she was also anticipating the possibility of another letter or card from Grandma Ev's sister, Lucille. Much to her delight, her house guest had arrived and they'd spent a wonderful afternoon together, but much to her disappointment, no letter had arrived.

Today, Fiona was once again looking forward to her time with Silja and rehearsing with Nathan, but she was feeling even more eager that perhaps a letter from yesteryear with more clues about the mysterious Lucille Stacy-Smith would arrive.

"Everything's set for Friday, right?" Bethann Mills, the school nurse asked, breaking through her thoughts.

"Friday?" Fiona repeated, blinking back into the moment and searching her mind for the Friday connection.

"Yeah, *Friday*—Principal Britton's birthday. You said you'd make the arrangements for the cake. I wrote the number for the bakery in Beaver for you on a sticky-note and put it in your backpack, remember? I put the note in there while you were lining your class up for afternoon bus calls. I told you where the note was. Anyway, Julia, the school *librarian*, said she'd pick the cake up on her way to school Friday morning. She lives near Beaver, I guess," Bethann explained with a hint of reprimand in her voice.

A surge of panic rushed through Fiona's gut. The sticky-note! The sticky-note she'd found in her backpack and threw away because she couldn't remember whose phone number was scribbled on it—it was the bakery! Ugh! That's right, she was supposed to order the cake, but she didn't!

Idiot!

In her own defense, it would have been most helpful if Bethann would have written the word, *bakery* on the note. Maybe it would have been really helpful if Bethann would have waited until bus calls were finished before she told her where she'd put the note. Okay, what was done, was done. No worries—or at least she *hoped* there were no worries. After all, she still had twenty-four hours before the cake was to be ready, but she needed to call the bakery like…*now*!

"You look pale. Are you okay?" Bethann asked.

"I'm fine—I just need to do something," Fiona said.

Crossing her arms over her chest, Bethann tossed her a baleful look. "You need to order the cake, don't you?"

"No! No…it's something far more urgent, like… like…I need to pee, right now," With that, Fiona rushed down the hall.

"724-555-8444!" Bethann called after her.

Busted.

Well, at least the mystery of the phone number on the sticky-note had been solved.

❧ ❧ ❧

Detective Landry rolled his SUV to a stop in front of a large Victorian-style home in the Squirrel Hill area of Pittsburgh. Turning off the ignition, he asked Yallowitz, "What made you guys so sure it was Di Volante in the burning car that night?"

"If my memory serves me right, Rowan found out that Di Volante was playin' cards with some friends in a house on Steuben Street—I'm thinkin' that may be where Angelo Moretti fits in. Anyways, we had the place pretty much surrounded, then Di Volante jumps out a window on the street side of the house and makes a run for a car parked at the curb. Shots were fired but he managed to jump in and drive off. Rowan, me, and a couple of the other guys took off after him. Like I said, we chased him for quite a way before he didn't maneuver a turn good enough, crashed and burned," Yallowitz explained.

"He jumped out of a window? The report said it was a door," Landry supplied.

"Nope. It was a window for sure…he was limpin' bad, prob'ly twisted his ankle, but boy, he could still run."

"Noted—so, why were you so sure you were chasing Di Volante?"

"Cuz the guys who were in the house said it was him. They didn't know why we were there, and they didn't know he had killed anyone, but they said he was definitely playin' cards with them and ran when he realized we were outside. Sure hope you didn't dig up a grave for nothin'—families really hate that. The media loves it, but the captain *really* hates it."

"Did you have a list of the names of the men who were playing cards with Di Volante that night?" Detective Landry asked.

Yallowitz shrugged. "Should'a been in the report."

"*Should'a* isn't gonna get me the list," Detective Landry groused.

"Hey, it wasn't *my* report to file. Rowan was the lead on that case. You know how it is, Landry, things get misplaced over the years. Old closed cases that become new cold cases are tough to crack because so much of the information is lost—like lists of witnesses, or the witnesses themselves disappear or die," Yallowitz pointed out.

Detective Landry opened the door to step out of the SUV. "Let's go talk with Izzy."

"*Izzy*? Sounds like you've already met her," Yallowitz said.

"I have. At the cemetery, when we were digging up the grave."

"Ya didn't tell me that."

"Ya didn't ask."

"Ya could'a still told me," Yallowitz said.

"And ruin the mystery of her good looks? No way."

"Well, is she still good-lookin'?"

"Beauty is in the eye of the beholder, Yallowitz," Detective Landry stated as they strolled up the sidewalk toward the grand old house.

"Nice cliché, Landry, I miss that about you," Yallowitz grumbled.

A light breeze drifted across the wraparound porch fashioned with white wicker chairs and fluffy blue floral pillows. Urns of bright pink impatiens flanked the front door. Baskets of huge leafy ferns hanging from chains over the porch railings floated on the waft. As Detective Landry pressed the doorbell, he noticed a fat white Persian cat stretched out on one of the wicker chairs, eyeing them.

The detective elbowed Yallowitz and hitched his chin toward the feline. "Security detail."

"The best kind," Yallowitz replied.

With a loud *creak*, the front door opened. Isadora Danza filled the doorway wearing a pair of cream flood pants, a long over-sized floral blouse, and a pair of blue ballet slip-ons. Her dark hair was pulled back in a severe bun, and pearl studs graced her lobes. She was void of the rhinestone sunglasses, yet nary a wrinkle was to be found around her eyes. She glanced at Landry then Yallowitz and back to Detective Landry.

Her Italian accent was more audible without the hindrance of a backhoe's engine. "Detective Landry, how nice to see you again. What can I do for you?"

"I hope we're not intruding, but I wanted to ask you a few questions, about Vincent Di Volante." He turned to gesture to Yallowitz who was staring at her like a love-sick teen. "I'm sure you probably don't remember, but this is Detective Norman Yallowitz. He worked the Di Volante case all those years ago." Smiling, she nodded in response. Landry wasn't sure if she was nodding to acknowledge the stoic Yallowitz or if she, in fact, did not remember him at all. "Um…anyway, do you mind if we come in to talk with you?"

"Of course. I was just about to have some tea. Can I pour you some?" Isadora asked.

"That would be nice, thanks," Landry replied.

She stepped aside to give them entry when she noticed the cat on the chair. "Stella, what are you doing out here? Come inside where you belong." She stepped onto the porch to gather the cat into her arms. Yallowitz held the door open for her, and she carried the cat into the living room. Before she set the cat's paws to a chair, she hugged the cat tightly and whispered in Italian, "*Dobbiamo stare attenti ora, amore mio.*" Smiling, Isadora gestured for the detectives to have a seat.

Detective Landry returned her smile, then took a seat on the couch.

A silver tray was stationed in the middle of the coffee table in the elegant room. A ceramic teapot decorated with daisies sat in the middle of the tray, while two matching teacups sat on either side of the pot along with a creamer and sugar bowl.

Detective Landry noticed a deep indent in the cushion on the other end of the couch where someone had been sitting not long ago. Yallowitz sat in a chair near the one the cat was lounging upon. Stella observed their every move wearing a wily gape. Isadora picked up the pot and began pouring the tea into the cups.

"You have a beautiful home, Ms. Danza. It's really big, do you live here alone?" Detective Landry inquired.

"Ugh. I need another teacup. Please excuse me, I'll be right back," Isadora said as she hurried toward a threshold that led out of the room, then she turned back. "Please,

Detective Landry, call me Izzy—I prefer it." With that, she made her exit.

Wearing a sly smirk, Yallowitz quietly remarked, "You've made a *big* impression, Landry."

Detective Landry hitched his chin toward the indent in the cushion. "So has someone else."

Yallowitz raised his eyebrows in reply.

Isadora returned to the room carrying a teacup. "I'm sorry, I don't remember your first name, Detective Landry."

"Nathan—"

"You should probably call him, Nate. That's what all his good friends call him," Yallowitz put in.

She tossed Yallowitz a svelte smile, then poured tea into the cups. She handed Detective Landry a cup. "What is it that you wanted to ask me, Nathan?" She gave Yallowitz a cup. "I'm not sure how I can help you. Vincent Di Volante has been dead for many years."

"Do you know a man named, Angelo Moretti?"

Isadora stilled. Her shoulders tensed. "What do you want to know about my brother?"

"Angelo Moretti was your brother?"

"My given name is, *Isabella* Moretti. I changed my name to Isadora Danza for the ballroom circuit. My father did not approve of the dancing. Angelo was older than me by ten years. My parents immigrated from Italy in the late 1930s. My brother was a babe in arms. They waited until they were more settled, here in the United States, before they conceived me. My dear brother passed away six months ago—heart attack."

"I'm sorry for your loss. Is that whose grave you were visiting when we met?" Detective Landry inquired.

"I was visiting Angelo, his wife, Katrina, and my parents of course. Angelo is buried next to my mother. He was very *dedicated* to them."

"I see, and you never married?"

Isadora took a long sip of her tea. "No…I never found the right one."

"Vincent Di Volante, was he one of your many suitors?" Detective Landry inquired.

Again, the corners of her lips lifted. "I'm flattered that you think there were *many* suitors, but no, Vincent and I were not involved back then. Yes, he was interested, but I was not, and then, of course, you are aware of what took place. It was a shame. Those young men were beautiful dancers. I still feel bad for what happened. Why are you asking about Angelo? What could he possibly have to do with Vincent?"

"Were Mr. Di Volante and your brother acquainted?" Detective Landry asked.

Isadora brushed back an errant strand of hair from her right eye. "They may have known one another, yes, but if so, I do not know what their relationship might have been. Angelo was a quiet man. He kept to himself. He did not share much about his life…even with me. As I said, he was very dedicated to the care of our parents. He honored their *every* request. He and his wife lived with them in their later years. Angelo was a very traditional Italian man in many, *many* ways."

"And your niece, Teresa, are you close with her?"

"Not really. I travel so much, and she is a very busy doctor. We exchange Christmas cards, an occasional email, but that's about all."

"I see," Detective Landry said. "It's strange, but the lead detective from that time, Detective Rowan, made note that both you and Mr. Di Volante came from immigrant parents. What an odd thing to make note of. Can you think of a reason he would've felt compelled to include that information in his report?"

"It was such a long time ago, Nathan. I don't remember my conversations with Detective Rowan. The notes you speak of belonged to him. Perhaps you should look him up and ask him these things."

Detective Landry stood while shaking his head. "He passed several years ago—cancer. Such a shame—ya work all those years, only to die a year or so into your retirement. It's like my mom always says, money is something we've gotta make—just in case we *don't* die."

Isadora chuckled. "Your mother is quite right."

He took her hand into his. "Thanks so much for your time, Ms. Danza—"

She pushed up from her seat. "*Izzy*—I wish you would call me, Izzy."

"It was a pleasure, ma'am," Yallowitz put in. He followed Detective Landry toward the door only to take a quick step back when Landry spun around.

"I hate to bring up your brother so close to his passing, Izzy, really I do, but did Angelo enjoy playing cards?"

"Oh my, yes. He and my father and some friends used to play cards for hours." Isadora replied with a smile in her voice—an obvious sweet memory.

"Thanks, I just wondered. Again, so sorry for your loss. Have a lovely rest of the day," the detective said, allowing Yallowitz to step out of the house, then closing the door behind him.

When they arrived back at Detective Landry's SUV, Yallowitz said, "That got us exactly nowhere."

"What are ya talkin' about? You got to see how beautiful Isadora Danza still is," Landry pointed out.

"Yeah, and I got to see how crazy she is about you."

"Whatever," Landry muttered, as he slid into the driver's seat and pulled the seatbelt over his shoulder. "We gotta find that list, Yallowitz. I'll bet my whole stinkin' retirement fund that Angelo Moretti's name is on it."

"May as well gamble your retirement away, like Rowan, ya might not live long enough to spend it anyways," Yallowitz grumbled.

SEVEN

S ilja rolled her eyes while tossing her hands in the air. "C'mon, you can't really be this wimpy, can you?" She was standing over Nathan and Fiona who were lying on the cool basement floor—flushed, sweaty, and gasping for air. "I'm surprised at you, Fiona. You used to dance for hours and that was after a two-hour barre workout—a *wicked* barre workout."

Between gasps, Fiona managed, "That was *ten* years ago. I'm older and wiser and obviously far more out of shape than I realized. Seriously, I need to hit the gym more than twice a week. Maybe I should add another yoga class on the weekends."

Silja shook her head. "And you, *Detective* Nathan Landry, I thought you'd be in better condition as well. Don't you have to run down the bad guys, haul them in, and throw the book at them?"

Before Nathan could get a word out, Fiona laughed. "Are you kidding? With all the chocolate and pizza and other junk this man ingests, his arteries are probably three-quarters of the way closed. He's lucky he hasn't had a heart attack already."

"Thanks for that vote of confidence, ladies. I'm totally whooped, beat, exhausted. And just for the record—I never run—*never*. I'm waiting for that moment I have to run for my life—I should have a lot of stamina saved up for that moment. Look, you're beautiful, Silja, but I don't know how Grant keeps up with you," Nathan said.

Silja chuckled. "Grant stays as far away from dance as he possibly can. He'd never attempt this stuff, so you get ten points for that, Nathan." She handed him a pair of aviator sunglasses. "Now, put these back on. We're going to start from the beginning. Fiona, make sure when you whip the glasses from his face, you throw them fairly far away so you don't trip over them."

"I was wondering about that. What about the other dancers?" Nathan asked.

"Guess they'll have to watch out, won't they? Silja replied.

Fiona pushed up to her elbows. "Okay, got it—toss sunglasses far away. Do you mind if I go upstairs for a moment? I want to go to the bathroom and I want to check on the mail."

"Oh! I forgot, I picked up the mail on my way in this afternoon," Silja began. "You didn't have much, but there was one very odd-looking envelope—"

Fiona shot to an upright position. "What? I had mail today? Where is it?"

"I carried it up to my room. I'm sorry, I must not have been paying attention—it's lying on the vanity—" Silja flinched when Fiona jumped to her feet to rush toward the stairs. Silja hurried after her, with Harriet on her heels. "Where are you going? Did I do something wrong?"

"No! I want to see that odd piece of mail. It's important," Fiona called over her shoulder. The stairs creaked beneath their hurried footsteps.

The basement door opened then slammed closed.

Quick moving footfalls thudded overhead. Still flat on his back, Nathan yelled toward the rafters above, "It's okay, just leave me here to die alone. No worries."

જી જી જી

Swiping several wet, stray strands of hair from her face, Fiona rushed into the guest bedroom with Silja close behind. Harriet dove onto the bed to dance in tiny circles while letting out a few fervent barks.

"There, on the vanity," Silja pointed out. "I'm so sorry, Fiona. I carried them upstairs, set them down, and forgot all about them. I had no idea you were waiting for something important to arrive."

"It's okay, to be honest, I wasn't sure I'd receive any more mail from my deceased great-aunt," Fiona said, now out of breath from climbing two staircases at a good pace. She grabbed the mail lying on the vanity, discarding several items before she came upon a yellowed envelope addressed to, Evelyn Burrell. Yep, the Dixmont postmark was present and accounted for.

"A letter from your *deceased* aunt? Okay, Quinn, this is starting to get a little *too* weird. What's going on?" Silja asked.

Fiona plopped down on the edge of the bed to tentatively open the aged envelope. Harriet sidled up to her right, while Silja eased down to peer over her left shoulder. "I've been receiving mail for my grandmother from her sister, Lucille, from *years* ago. I received a letter a day or so ago and I thought maybe I wouldn't get any more, but here's another one."

"You didn't tell me you got another letter," Nathan said.

The girls looked up to see him leaning against the jamb. Sweat soaked his gray T-shirt with FBI scrolled across the chest. Fiona said, "I'm sorry, with Silja arriving and all the rehearsals, I guess I forgot to mention it."

"So, you've received a *letter* since the Christmas card?" Nathan inquired.

"Uh, huh."

"What did it say?" Nathan asked.

"Basically, Lucille was asking my grandmother for help, but she didn't exactly say what she needed. She also mentioned that Gram was the only one she could trust. Unfortunately, Gram never received her letter or should I say, *letters*, and now this one has arrived. I was hoping Gram had received others. Sadly, it appears she did not."

"So, you're saying that Grandma Evie is receiving letters from years and years ago that were never delivered? Until now? Here? At *your* house?" Silja verified.

"That's right," Fiona replied.

"That's *so* freaky," Silja said.

"I know, right?" Checking the envelope, Fiona noted, "This one is postmarked 1976."

"Wait…Silja knows about Grandma Ev's ghost?" Nathan asked.

"Um…well…yes. But Silja has known for quite some time. She has history with my grandmother—"

"Never mind. I get it," Nathan said as he crossed the room to sit on the bed next to Fiona, placing Harriet on his lap. "Okay, let's see what Lucille has to say this time."

Silja rubbed her hands up and down her arms rapidly. "I've got goosebumps."

Fiona carefully slipped the letter from the envelope. "This one is a bit more wrinkled than the other one." She paused to study the note. "And, the handwriting is even more slanted—almost erratic—than the last. She tends to press down really hard on her pencil, and look—" She pointed to a dark smudge on the page. "It looks like the pencil may have broken at this point in the letter. Is she under more duress than before?" Fiona exchanged glances with Nathan and then with Silja. Taking in a calming breath, she continued, "Anyway, she says, Dear Evelyn, why haven't you answered my letter? Where is Ed? He hasn't been to visit in two weeks. Is he plotting against me to take my children away? Why hasn't he come? Please, Ev, write back. Your loving sister, Lucille."

Letting out a sigh, Fiona dropped her hands to her lap. The small group sat in silence for a moment. Nathan quietly asked, "May I see the letter?" Without looking up from her lap, she handed him the page. He examined it for a moment. "You're right, she does press down very hard on her pencil, and it looks like it broke off right here—where she mentions that Ed, her husband, hasn't visited in two weeks. Frustration."

"I can totally understand why she's frustrated. She's locked up in that gawd-awful place. It sounds like she's not exactly sure where all her children are, no one will talk to her, and she's starting to think her family is turning on her. This is a tragedy. I feel so bad. My heart is broken for her. I'm sad for my grandmother too," Fiona said.

Wiping a tear from her cheek, Silja asked, "What did this woman do that they put her in a mental institution?"

"We really don't know. The letters are from so long ago, and Dixmont has been closed up and torn down since about 1984," Nathan supplied. He examined the postmark. "This is dated April of '76. What was the date on the other letter you received?"

"I believe the year was 1976, but I don't remember the month." Fiona lifted her gaze to meet Nathan's. "Don't you think it's strange? How are the cards and letters finally getting here, and why? My grandmother didn't live here, with us, until the late 1990's—she was still living in her little house over on Guyland Street. Grandma didn't move in with us until I was about twelve. So why would the mailman bring the letters *here*?"

Nathan shrugged. "The mailman knows you live here. He probably knows Evelyn Burrell was your grandmother. Didn't you say he graduated with you or something to that effect?"

"Jason Gardner is our *new* mailman—he started about a year or so ago. He was a year ahead of me, but yes, we both attended Langley High. I think I'm going to make a point to drop by several of my neighbor's houses to see if they're getting this stuff, then I'm going to Jason's house and see what's going on with all this old mail," Fiona said.

"Not a bad idea. In the meantime, I'm gonna see if I can find out what happened to Edward Smith. Do you mind if I have a look at the other letter? I'd like to see the date of that postmark."

"Um…sure—"

Nathan held up his hand. "Let me guess—you put the letter upstairs so your grandmother could read it."

Silja let out a loud snort. "You two are meant to be together! He knows you *sooo* well, my dear, Fiona."

Fiona let out a sigh. "Am I that transparent?"

"Yes!" Silja and Nathan said in unison, then laughed.

"Alrighty, then. Let's go upstairs to get the last letter and leave this one behind for her to take a look at, when and if she's ready." Fiona pushed up from the bed and headed for the bedroom door. They crossed the small foyer, and Fiona opened the door to the staircase that led to the third-floor apartment. When she opened the door, a cold breeze wafted down the stairwell. "Whoa, that's strange. These stairs are usually super-hot this time of the year."

As the trio climbed the enclosed staircase, the air grew colder rather than warmer. Harriet lagged behind the small group. When she reached the top, Fiona flicked on the light, and much to her surprise, the middle drawer in Grandma Ev's desk was wide open. The letter she'd placed in the drawer on top of the old Christmas cards was lying on the floor, crumpled up. Fiona shivered. The room was freezing cold as if it were twenty-degrees outside rather than seventy-two.

Nathan and Silja stepped onto the third floor to look over Fiona's shoulder, while Harriet sat down at Fiona's feet—it was almost as if the little dog wasn't sure if she should enter the apartment area.

"Whoa, did you leave the air on up here? It's freezing," Silja said while running her hands up and down her arms.

"Um, Nathan opened a window to let some air in, but it hasn't been this cold outside," Fiona supplied. "How very odd."

"Is that the letter?" Nathan asked, gesturing to the paper on the floor.

"I think it might be," Fiona murmured, as she inched her way toward the crumpled note. With slow measured movements, she bent down to touch the paper with gentle fingertips, then pulled her hand to her chest. Around a quiet gasp, she said, "It's wet. Well, not exactly wet, it's kind of…moist."

"Maybe because it's so cold up here? Could it be condensation?" Silja inquired.

Looking tentatively around the room, Nathan ambled toward Fiona, then bent down to touch the paper. "You're right, it's very moist, but I don't think it's condensation." Fiona met his gaze. "I'm no expert, and Lord knows, I didn't know your grandma personally, but…is it possible…could the wetness be—"

"Tears?" Fiona suggested. As delicately as she could manage, she lifted the letter from the floor and unfolded the furrowed paper. She cupped her hand over her mouth. After a moment, she moved her hand to her chest. "Oh, the dampness smeared some of the handwriting." She glanced around the room, then went to the desk to pick up the envelope lying on the desktop. "It's funny, Gram is a spirit, and yet she doesn't seem to be in touch with Lucille. As disturbing as this entire situation is, you'd think Lucille would want to connect with Gram. Unless…she was so upset by the lack of communication before she died that she is feeling bitter toward her sister—even though this wasn't Gram's fault at all. You wanted to see the envelope for the postmark—here it is."

"You could be on to something." Nathan eased the envelope from Fiona's shaking hand. "Go downstairs with Silja. I'll take it from here."

Fiona looked into his eyes. She couldn't be sure what she was seeing, but he was steadfast in his request. What was Nathan planning to do? She couldn't begin to guess, but she knew one thing for sure—whatever it was, he was committed to it. Worried about Grandma Ev's reaction to the first letter, she nodded her compliance, scooped Harriet into her arms, and followed Silja down the stairs.

Nathan stood quietly in the middle of Grandma Ev's former apartment until he heard the door that led into the second-floor foyer close. He took in a breath and then looked up to the ceiling. "Hey, Grandma Ev, it's me, Nathan. I gotta admit I'm a little surprised, I would've thought your sister would'a told you what happened to her before she died…er…since yinzer both dead and all. Then again, I have no idea how Heaven works." He ran his left hand up and down his right arm. "In any case, I can't change what happened all those years ago, but I'm gonna find out what happened to Edward, and if at all possible, what happened to Lucille too."

Making his way to the stairs, he studied the envelope in his hand. The Dixmont postmark was dated April 30, 1976. He stopped at the staircase and looked back. "I promise to get to the bottom of this, Ev. Oh, and by the way, I'm not just doing this for you. I'm doing it for Lucille and my Fiona—I sure do love that girl." Without warning, a warm breeze blew through the apartment to ruffle his hair. He favored the room with a smile and a nod. "All right then."

EIGHT

Fiona and Silja walked across Oxford Street to Pat McCune's home. Pat and her husband, Steve, had been lifelong neighbors. The McCune's were older than her parents—well into their seventies. She and her husband had raised two sons and a daughter. Nowadays, only Pat and her husband lived in the split-entry home. Fiona's neighbor, Astrid, had mentioned that Pat had been on the receiving end of some of the belated mail. Fiona was hoping Pat could tell her if other neighbors were getting the delayed mail too.

Pat's green eyes brightened and a smile stretched across her face when she opened the door to find Fiona on the stoop. "Fiona, how nice to see you. How are your parents doing? I'll bet they love living in Florida, don't they?" She turned to call over her shoulder. "Steve… Fiona Quinn's here to visit, pour some iced tea. Come in, sweetheart, come in." She stepped aside to give Fiona entry. Upon laying eyes on Fiona's friend, Pat added,

"Steve, Fiona's got a little friend with her. We need *four* glasses of tea, please."

"Do you think they'll give us a lollipop before we leave?" Silja whispered in Fiona's ear.

Around a snort, Fiona gently elbowed her, then followed Pat up the stairs into the living room. No more than a moment later, Steve shuffled into the room carrying a tray with four glasses of iced tea. Pat gestured for the girls to sit, so they eased onto the couch. Steve proceeded to hand out the tea, then he sat down in a chair near the front window. Pat sat on the arm of Steve's chair.

"This is my friend, Silja Ramsay. We used to dance at Pittsburgh Ballet together. Anyway, the reason I stopped by was because I was talking with Astrid Dingle the other day and she told me you had received a birthday card from your mom from many years ago," Fiona said.

"Oh, yes, I received a birthday card, that was several days ago," Pat replied.

"Tell them what you got in the card, Patty," Steve said.

Pat chuckled. "It was a birthday card with twenty dollars in it."

"It had twenty bucks in it. How do you like that?" Steve asked.

Fiona giggled. "I'd like that very much, thank you."

"Astrid said you've been receiving mail too," Pat said.

"Yes, we heard you got some old mail too," Steve added.

"I have," Fiona began. "That's what I wanted to talk to you about. Have you received just the one birthday card or have you received more since then?"

Pat shook her head. "No, nothing else."

"No, she hasn't gotten anything else," Steve reiterated.

"Of course, my mother lived in Crafton Heights. I saw her all the time when she was living, so there was no real need for her to mail anything other than a birthday card or a Christmas card. I heard Peggy Krebs and Carol Campbell received some of that older mail too. I can't imagine what took it so long to get delivered," Pat explained.

"No, her mom didn't send much mail our way. 'Course, she lived so close by—" Steve clarified.

"Have you met our new mailman? His name is Jason. He's a very nice boy," Pat said.

"Oh, yes, our new mailman, Jason, is very nice indeed," Steve agreed.

Fiona pushed up from her seat, and Silja jumped to her feet too. "Well, that's exactly who I'm planning to visit, Jason Gardner. Maybe he can shed some light on where this mail is coming from, or why it's so late being delivered."

҂ ҂ ҂

Detective Landry rolled his SUV to a stop in front of Isadora Danza's home. Turning off the ignition, he glanced down the lengthy sidewalk that led to the large Victorian house. He pulled a bite-size Snickers from his pocket, unwrapped it, and tossed it into his mouth.

His cell phone rang.

He picked the cell up from the cupholder, pressed the button, and held it to his ear. Around a mouthful of chocolate, he said, "Landry…"

"You were right," he heard the captain say. "I just got a call from the coroner. The body you had exhumed yesterday was not Vincent Di Volante."

"Who was it?"

"Dunno. And he said they won't know for a while. They're way backed-up. Prob'ly won't have an ID for a week or so."

Stepping out of the SUV, the detective said, "Good enough. I'll work with what I've got." Ending the call and stuffing the phone in his pocket, he made his way up the sidewalk and onto the porch. He glanced around at the wicker chairs and the railing—no cat. He rang the bell and a few moments later, Isadora opened the door.

"Nathan, what a lovely surprise. Please, come in. I'm always thrilled when I have a handsome guest, like you," Isadora said, smiling.

The detective was a bit taken aback when she ran her fingers across his shoulder as he stepped through the door into the foyer. "I hope I'm not intruding, Ms. Danza—"

"*Izzy*," she insisted around an exaggerated pout.

"Izzy… I just wanted to ask you a few questions about the night Vincent Di Volante died."

She gestured toward the seats in the living room. "Have a seat, Nathan. I was just about to pour some tea. Won't you have some?"

"Well—"

"I insist. It is such a treat for an older woman, such as myself, to spend time with such a handsome younger man," she explained.

"Well—" Just then there was a crash somewhere in the house—it sounded as if glass had shattered on a floor. His instinct kicking in, Detective Landry moved forward, but Isadora waved a careless hand.

"Please don't be concerned. That mischievous cat of mine is always breaking things. Please, have a seat. I'll get the tea."

"Do you need help cleaning up a mess?"

"Heavens no. You're my guest, Nathan. I'll be back in a moment." With that, she made her exit. Her movements as elegant as Ginger Rogers herself.

The detective made his way around the living room perusing the photographs on the end tables, the mantel, and the cherry bookcase on the far wall. Each and every image was of Isadora at different stages of her life sporting beautiful flowing, sassy fringed, or skimpy sequined ballroom attire. In each photo, the dancer's expression and body position were purposely animated in an intensely dramatic manner.

The images were amazing—breathtaking.

The detective lifted one of the many 8X10 crystal frames from the bookcase to take a closer look, and there *he* was—Isadora's arcane dance partner. Pulling the lone photograph, he'd retained of Vincent Di Volante, he found it most interesting that even though this was her private estate—her personal collection of memorabilia— this particular partner's identity was kept hidden. He noted that none of the photos featured any other partner. This constant partner was either shot from behind or was faced away from the camera. Regardless, he compared his aged photo of Di Volante to the man in the many pictures stationed about the room.

From the other room, Isadora's voice broke his muse. She was speaking in Italian, but he could not make out her words—she was talking quietly, yet no one replied. A nanosecond later, she stepped into the room with a small tray filled with a porcelain teapot and cups.

"Here we are. A nice fresh pot of tea," she said, making her way toward the coffee table. She straightened, narrowing her eyes. "What are you doing?"

Placing the frame back into its place, the detective said, "Your photographs are quite impressive, beautiful. I don't think my girl and I look *that* good when we're taking our lessons."

After setting the tray on the table, Isadora clapped her hands merrily. "You are still taking classes, how wonderful. You will never regret learning to dance and dancing the tango or the mambo with your lover can be quite... exhilarating, sensual."

Landry snorted. "I'm not sure how exhilarating it is—it's more...clumsy than anything else, but we're still at it." Feeling a bit ill at ease with the direction of the conversation, he put his hand up. "Not to change the subject, but, who is this guy in the pictures?"

Isadora cocked her head to one side. "Which picture?"

With a sweep on his right hand, Detective Landry gestured to all of the areas where the photos were stationed. "All of the pictures. Is it the same guy? It looks to me like it's the same guy. 'Course, I could be wrong. I find it rather strange that his face is not shown in any of the photographs. Still, it looks like the same guy." He held up the photo of Vincent Di Volante. "I think he looks a lot like, Vincent Di Volante."

Isadora waved a flippant hand. "Those are photographs of me. I had the pictures taken for the program books that are handed out at the competitions. The dancers often have these photos taken and placed in the books for the judges to see. It is…um…an advertisement or a marketing tool, if you will, for the dancers to be noticed. Those pictures are from many years ago, of course."

"I see. But why is his face not shown?"

Isadora busied herself with pouring tea into the cups. "Because the photos are to promote me, not him."

"Ahhh, does it work?"

"Yes. Yes, it works very well." She gestured to the couch. "Please, Nathan, sit."

"Who is the man?"

"Honestly, it was such a long time ago, I simply don't remember."

"Are ya sure? Are ya sure that's not Vincent Di Volante?"

She stilled, then shook her head. "It may be. I posed with whoever was available. Whoever the photographer managed to grab."

"That's surprising. I would think the dancers would be falling over each other to pose with you. You were so beautiful and such a dancer in demand," Detective Landry put in.

Plopping her hands on her hips, Isadora raised her brows. "I *was* beautiful? I'm broken-hearted, Nathan."

He snorted. "You are still *very* beautiful."

"Thank you. Now, come have some tea."

He crossed the room. She handed him a cup. "Thanks."

That's when he noticed a bite-size Snickers on the tray next to the teapot. She tossed him a flirty smile. Picked up the candy, ripped the wrapper, tossed the paper to the tray, broke the tiny piece of chocolate in half, and then dropped one half into her cup of tea and the other into his cup. "Like you, we Italians love our chocolate." She raised her voice just a bit. "And we Italian women prefer *younger* men, too."

"Isadora…I mean, *Izzy*, did your brother play cards with Vincent Di Volante?"

"I cannot lie to you, Nathan. That would be wrong. I believe, yes, Angelo did play cards with Vincent."

He took a sip of the tea. "So, they knew each other?"

"I believe so."

"Hm. I thought you said before that you weren't sure."

"I was wrong. I do think they knew each other."

"Did your brother play cards with Vincent the night he died?"

"Why do you fuss over a dead man, Nathan? Why do you pick at his remains?" Isadora asked.

He peered at her over his teacup. "Do *you* believe he's dead, Isadora?"

She let out a thin gasp. "Of course, he is. He has been dead for many years. You haven't found out otherwise, have you?"

"We're still working on it. These things take time, ya know. I really should be going."

"What's the rush? You have barely touched your tea."

Pushing up from the couch, the detective set the cup on the coffee table. "Police stuff." She followed him into the foyer. Almost to the door, he hesitated and turned toward her. "One more thing—the guy in the photographs—"

Stepping around him, she opened the door. "What guy?"

"The one in all your dance pictures—the one whose face is never shown."

She shrugged. "What about him?"

"You're absolutely sure he's not Di Volante?" the detective pressed.

Isadora raised a careless shoulder. "I told you, those were promotional photographs of me. He…he was another dancer who agreed to pose with me at the time, and that was a long time ago. I suppose he could be Vincent. I needed the pictures. At the time, I really didn't care who I posed with."

"For the program books at the competitions?"

"That is correct, my dear inquisitive, but so handsome, Nathan," Isadora replied.

The detective stepped through the door. "Boy, I sure would like to see one of those books. I'll bet my girl would too—it would give us something to work toward. Not that we'd ever reach that level of dance, mind you. Would you happen to have one lying around?"

Isadora stilled. She averted her gaze and raised her chin. "I'm sure that I do…somewhere…in a box…in the attic, back in a corner—"

"That's too bad. They sure are impressive pictures. I'll bet that guy had his picture taken too, with a pretty dancer, so the judges would notice him too. Do ya think?"

She brushed an errant hair from her face, then replied, "Maybe. I'm not sure. If I should come across the books, I'll let you know."

"That would be great. Well, thanks for the tea, and the talk." He started across the porch, then glanced at her over his shoulder. "*Arrivederci*, Izzy."

"Ciao, bello."

NINE

Fiona rolled her Mini Cooper to a stop in front of a brick house on Stratmore Street. She turned toward Silja in the passenger seat. "This is it. This is where Jason lives. I hope he's home, and I hope he has answers to our questions." Just then her cell phone rang. "Hello…"

"Hey, Fiona, I'm gonna pick up a movie for tonight. You girls want a comedy?" Nathan asked.

"Sounds good. We're trying on my ballroom dresses this afternoon. I'm starting to get a little nervous, Nathan, how about you?"

"Don't worry about a thing, darlin'. You'll be great. I'm getting the strangest vibes from Isadora Danza's house—every time I go there, it feels like there's someone else in the house."

Fiona snorted. "Hm. You've always felt that way every time you come to my house too, and you were right. I'd trust my gut, if I were you, Detective Landry."

"Yeah, that's what I'm thinkin'. I'll see ya later tonight. Can't wait to see what you look like all dressed up like a ballroom dancer."

With a smile in her voice, Fiona said, "Bye, Nathan." She disconnected the call and slipped from the car.

Silja slid out of the car to follow Fiona toward the house. "Does Jason, the mail-guy, have a wife?"

"I'm not sure. He might."

"Hm, I wonder if she'll repeat everything he says," Silja put in around a snort.

Cocking her head to one side while tossing her friend a baleful look, Fiona pressed the doorbell. "I think the McCune's are *adorable*. In fact, they put me in mind of what you and Grant will be like when you're old."

Silja returned Fiona's smirk. "Very funny."

"You're just mad because you didn't get a lollipop."

"Got me."

Just then the door opened. The sound of a television chattering in the background wafted out the door, as a tall gangly man filled the doorway. He had bright red hair and freckles covered his face. He was sporting a postman's uniform worn during the summer months: blue shorts, a blue shirt that was untucked and unbuttoned to reveal the white T-shirt he was wearing underneath, tall black socks, and black shoes. "Hey! Fiona! I haven't seen you in years. How've ya been?" Jason Gardner enveloped Fiona into his arms and squeezed tightly.

When he finally let go and she was able to step away from the embrace, Fiona managed, "Good to see you too, Jason. Congratulations on getting Mr. Bixby's position. Honestly, I thought he'd be our postman forever."

"Yeah, me too. Thanks. I just got home and was getting' ready to crack open a beer. Want one?"

"Um, no, but thank you. Actually, I'm here to ask about—"

"The old mail you've been getting? Yeah, I have no idea what that's about. But it's pretty cool, huh?" He turned toward the interior of the house. "Hey, Mom! How long has that mail been in our basement?"

Fiona and Silja exchanged glances—guess that answered the, is there a wife in the picture, question.

"Since your father and I moved here," his mother called from somewhere inside.

He turned back toward Fiona. "When I got Mr. Bixby's job, Mom told me about the bags of old mail that's been in our basement for like…forever. She showed me where it was stored. I did some research on our house and turns out another mailman lived here a long time ago— Theodore Bixby, Mr. Bixby's dad. Pretty weird. Anyway, I guess the old guy was on the loopy side and ended up having a nervous breakdown. Guess he couldn't handle the fact that the mail just keeps on comin', and comin', and comin'—no matter what. I guess he just quit delivering it. He was stuffing the mail bags in the fruit cellar in this house—there were dozens of them. I guess Mr. Bixby never told anyone because he didn't want to get his dad in trouble—Federal offense and all that stuff. Mom said Dad considered burning it, but he never got around to it, or maybe he couldn't bring himself to do it. Anyways, I started going through it and thought it was only right to deliver it—even if some of the people have been dead for a long time—like your grandma."

"So, let me get this straight. The mailman just *stopped* delivering the mail back in 1975 or 1976?" Fiona clarified.

"Yup." Jason rubbed the nape of his neck. "Can't say as I blame him much. Seriously, there are days the mail can be super overwhelming—especially around the holidays. Not just Christmas, mind you, Valentine's Day and Mother's Day can be real killers for the post office. I feel bad, but, I gotta admit, I threw some of that old stuff out—junk mail or mail that was so damaged from basement condensation I couldn't read who the recipient was anyways. I don't exactly know what to do with the mail for people who I know for sure have passed away, and I have no idea where their family members are—if they're still living. I've still got a few bags left too. I'll be glad when it's all gone, I can tell ya that."

"So, there could be more?" Fiona asked.

He shrugged. "I suppose so. Did ya get anything important? I've had a few customers tell me they got money and stuff. How about you?"

"I've received some rather important letters for my grandmother that I so wish she would've been able to read on time. It's too late now, and I'm not sure how things would've turned out had she received them when she should have." Fiona sighed. "Listen, Jason, if you find any more letters for my grandmother could you let me know immediately. Not that there's anything I or anyone else can do about what happened all those years ago, but—"

"I think I understand. Look, I go through one or two bags every weekend. If I find anything for Mrs. Burrell,

I'll call ya. I don't know what went on, but I can see it's important to you. I remember Mrs. Burrell. She was such a nice lady."

"Thanks, Jason. I appreciate it."

∽ ∽ ∽

When Detective Landry returned to his car and slid into the driver's seat, his cell phone rang. Around a careworn sigh, he dug the phone from his pocket and lifted it to his ear. "Landry…"

"Got a bit of bad news for ya, Nate."

"Tavia! You're back!"

"Of course, I'm back. It's a broken ankle—how long did you think I'd be off? 'Course, I'm on total desk duty until the ankle's healed. Anyway, I was doing some extra research for the captain and found that Vincent Di Volante does, in fact, have a living family member."

The detective fell back against his seat. "Uh, oh, the girl who was working your desk didn't find that for me."

"She was a newbie. Anyway, Di Volante has an older sister, Maria Francesco. She lives in Albany, New York. I spoke with her. She's madder than a wet hen that you've disturbed her brother. The captain said *you* have to deal with her, and if she goes to the media—you have to deal with *them*. I'll text you her number. Looks like you're up to your elbows in alligators, Detective."

"Really? I think this looks like a huge break in my case. Hey, speaking of breaks, can you do a little intel for me?"

He could hear her let out a big sigh on the other end. "Why am I not surprised? What do you need?"

"I need you to find out what happened to a woman named, Lucille Stacy-Smith. She did some time in the old Dixmont State Institution starting in 1975. I am also looking for her husband, Edward Smith."

"*Smith*? C'mon, *seriously*? Their name is *Smith*? Nice. There's only gotta be about a *billion* people named, Edward Smith and I'll just bet half of them live in Pittsburgh."

"Yeah, but how many Lucille Smiths' will you find who died in Dixmont around 1976?"

"I suppose."

"Oh, and one more thing—"

"Of course, there's one more thing...there's *always* one more thing."

"I'm looking for a list from this case. It's a list of men who were playing cards at the home on Stueben Street where Di Volante was *allegedly* found. I'm fairly sure you'll find the name, Angelo Moretti on the list, but I'd sure like to know who else was there."

"Anything else? A blood sample from my right arm? My first-born child?"

"No, I think that about covers it. Hey, welcome back, Tav."

"Gee, thanks. Oh, by the way, you received a recording."

"A recording?"

"Yes, from...let me see... Jefferson Memorial Cemetery."

"Whoa, that took a long time to get here," the detective groused.

"Looks like it has been here for a day or so. Maybe Amanda forgot to let you know."

"Well, I guess I know now. Thanks, Tav." He disconnected the call, then looked to Tavia's text message to fetch Maria Francesco's telephone number. The woman may be angry he exhumed her brother's body, but the fact was, he had some good news for her: Vincent was not in the grave. Mrs. Francesco would either be happy with the news…or not. He dialed her number, and the phone began to ring.

"Hello…"

"Hello, Mrs. Francesco, I'm Detective Nathan Landry, Pittsburgh Homicide. How are you today?"

Maria Francesco's voice sounded elderly. Detective Landry had her figured for about seventy-eight or so, considering Vincent Di Volante would most likely be in his mid-seventies. Like Isadora, she spoke with a slight Italian accent. "I'm extremely unhappy, Detective. How dare you disturb my poor brother without my permission. In fact, I was just getting ready to retain an attorney to sue your police department, and possibly, you *personally* as well—"

"Well, Mrs. Francesco, I understand your frustration. But before you get knee-deep in all that paperwork, and before you pay any hefty retainers, let me inform you that as far as we know, your brother is still alive. Or at least, he was not occupying the grave at Jefferson Memorial."

There was a long pause. He could almost hear Maria Francesco picking her jaw up from the floor. She stammered, "W-what are you talking about?"

"Upon the coroner's examination, the body we exhumed from Vincent Di Volante's grave was not that of Vincent Di Volante."

Another long pause. It was most obvious Maria Francesco was trying to wrap her head around the fact that her brother was still walking the earth. He knew exactly what she was thinking: how could that be?

He heard her swallow hard, and then she managed, "Well, tell me, Detective Landry, who in God's name was in my brother's grave, and where is my brother now?"

"We have yet to identify the body, and even if I did know the identity, I would not be at liberty to give you that information—at least, not until next of kin was notified. As for your brother, we are in the process of looking for him. By your reaction, I'm assuming you have not heard from him since 1976?"

"No—of course I haven't. I thought Vincent was dead. Like everyone else in our family, I believed he died in that fiery crash all those years ago. My parents went to their graves thinking they'd see him on the other side—and now, you claim he's still among us?"

"I'm afraid so. Do you—"

"It's all that woman's fault! I said it back then, and I'm saying it now, Isabella Moretti broke her parent's heart by not honoring their agreement with the Di Volante family, and my brother paid for her impertinence with his life!" The woman let out a whimper. The detective knew she was struggling to keep her emotions in check, and she was losing the fight.

"I'm so sorry I've upset you, Mrs. Francesco, but I need to know what happened all those years ago. The information you give me may help me to locate your brother."

"The Moretti family and the Di Volante family were very close. They came to America together. Our fathers, Vincent's and Isabella's, made an agreement when the two were born that they would marry. Our families would be joined forever through the marriage and grandchildren. But Isabella would not! No! She changed her name because she wanted to *dance*. She wanted to flit around the country like a—" Maria took in a deep calming breath. It took her a few moments to collect her composure. Nathan was fairly sure he heard her take a drink. Finally, she continued, "My brother took up the dancing so he could be near her. He thought he could coax her into loving him enough to please our parents, or at the very least, *her* parents. Angelo, Isabella's brother, tried to reason with her. Still, Isabella would not. She refused to have anything to do with Vincent. She would not even dance with him—at least not very often. She tried his patience to the extreme."

"I see. So, you're saying Vincent was jealous of Isadora's, I mean, *Isabella's* boyfriends or the dancers paired up with her at the competitions?"

"How could you blame him? She flaunted her beauty. The other men wanted to dance with her, as did Vincent. But she—" Maria's voice fell away. He could hear her sniffling into a tissue.

"But she, what, Mrs. Francesco?" the detective urged.

"Isabella was a flirt. A terrible, *terrible* flirt. Before Vincent's accident, it was rumored she'd taken up with a man, and the relationship was serious. Vincent was furious. Angelo said she was considering marrying this man, but there was some sort of problem. Angelo had told Vincent once the problem was solved, they were to be married. The night of the crash, Vincent went to Angelo's home...they were going to play cards with friends. He told Vincent he would bring Isabella so he could talk to her. I'm not sure what went wrong in that house, but Vincent ended up being chased by the police. They forced him to crash his car. It exploded and he was burned to death—or at least, we *thought* that is what happened."

"Yes, ma'am. You wouldn't happen to know who else was at the house playing cards, would you?"

She was quiet for a moment. "No, Detective, I'm sorry, I really don't know who Vincent's friends were—they may have been Angelo's friends."

Detective Landry knew he needed to proceed with extreme care. "Um...were you aware that several of the dancers who were paired with Isabella had been murdered?"

"Yes...I know the police *thought* Vincent was responsible for these men's deaths. Not *our* Vincent. He could not do such a thing—not even for Isabella's affections. *No.* I never believed this—nor did my parents."

"Thank you, Mrs. Francesco. I appreciate you talking with me."

"Detective...if you find Vincent..." Her feeble voice faltered into nothing.

"Yes, ma'am, if we find your brother, we will certainly notify you."

"Tell me…does Isabella still dance? I…I know she is quite aged by this time, but is she still active?"

"Yes, Mrs. Francesco, she is still quite active in the ballroom dance circuit. But I believe she is more in the role of a judge than a competitor these days."

"Thank you, Detective. I don't know how to feel. I don't know whether to be joyful that my brother may still be living or to be angry with his deception," Maria said around a whimper.

"I totally understand, ma'am. And again, thank you for all your help." With that, Detective Landry ended the connection. He shook his head. "Poor woman."

TEN

Wincing, Fiona sucked in a breath. "Ugh! Ah, *c'mon*, I don't remember my ballet costumes being this tight or this *itchy!*" She glanced down from the step stool on which she stood, while Silja attempted to zip up a bright-red, fringed and sequined, mambo dress. "This dress is way too short and way too... skimpy. Nathan and everyone in the audience are going to see everything I own."

Silja stepped back to look her friend over. "Perfect! You look fabulous." She took Fiona's hand and helped her down from the stool so she could look in the full-length mirror they'd dragged up from the basement.

Fiona's eyes widened. "Yikes!"

Silja rolled her eyes. "*Honestly,* you're such a *kindergarten* teacher. You're completely covered and because the dress is so tightly fitted, it will move with you—kind of like a second skin. No-one, *including Nathan*, will see anything except how gorgeous you are." She turned to retrieve a box from a nearby chair where Harriet was snoozing. "Here, try these on. I got these when I went out the other day—a pair of ruby-red dancing shoes to match the dress. The heels aren't too high, so you shouldn't kill yourself in the middle of the routine. Size six, right?" Nodding her head, yes, Fiona sat on the chair next to Harriet to open the box and slip into the bright-red shoes. Squealing, Silja clapped her hands in delight. "Oh! My God! You look *amazing*! They'll have to give you first-place just because you're so gorgeous!"

With her thumbs tucked into each side of the dress, Fiona pulled and tugged at the sequined straps. "Okay, let's move onto the waltz gown—I think I'll like that dress better." She twisted and turned in an attempt to unzip the scratchy garment.

Silja lifted a flowing blue-sequin dress that she'd draped over the couch. "I always loved my waltz gown—very elegant. You do know the mambo competition is first, right?"

Fiona blew out an anxious breath. "Yeah. I'm starting to get some serious butterflies in my belly. I hope this goes the way Nathan is planning. Maybe we won't even get as far as the dance-floor. Maybe he'll spot Vincent Di Volante right away and nab him quickly."

"He told me Isadora Danza is one of the judges for the competition. Isn't she the one he was supposedly killing the other dancers over?"

"I think so."

"Well then, there's probably a good chance that man will show up at the competition. In fact, there's a good chance he's been stalking her for years. Scary."

Fiona managed to wiggle out of the red mambo dress and toss it on the chair over a sleeping Harriet. The dress bumped and jerked about as if a red ghost were seated in the chair. At last, Harriet managed to peek out from under. Staring at the little dog struggling to free herself, but not really seeing her, Fiona murmured, "Stockholm Syndrome…Hm. I have to wonder…."

"Stockholm Syndrome?"

"Yeah, Stockholm Syndrome is when someone is taken prisoner and they actually form feelings of trust or even romance for their captors. They'll even protect them against the police—this happens a lot with abuse victims. Children will oftentimes protect an abuser and women will defend an abusive husband or lover when the police come to check on a disturbance," Fiona explained as she stepped into the waltz gown Silja was holding up for her.

Silja zipped the dress up. "So, you think Isadora Danza is somehow protecting this Vincent guy?"

"Could be. It's an interesting concept anyway." She looked in the mirror. "Hey, I like this dress much better."

Stepping back to take in Fiona's look, Silja expelled a charmed sigh. "Ah, you look absolutely enchanting. I can't wait until tomorrow."

"I can," Fiona groaned.

༄ ༄ ༄

Fiona fidgeted on the couch while Silja and Nathan ate popcorn from the large green and white mixing bowl that used to belong to Grandma Ev. Fiona simply could not relax. She could not find a comfortable spot on the couch, and she certainly couldn't eat. Nathan and Silja were having a grand time laughing at the movie Nathan had brought over for the evening. Meanwhile, Harriet was entertaining them with her silly antics while trying to cajole them into tossing popcorn for her to catch in her mouth.

Fiona was not amused.

Fiona's stomach was in knots.

Fiona was trying to quell her rising anxiety.

Fiona was failing, miserably.

At last, she could take no more. "How can the two of you be so calm when there's so much at stake tomorrow?" Yikes, she didn't mean to snap at them, but that's exactly how her question came out...as a big old *snap*.

Ouch.

Nathan turned toward her. "What's going on, Fiona? You've been restless all night. What's wrong?"

Letting out a haggard sigh, Fiona fell back against the couch. "I'm sorry. I just can't relax, what if things don't go as planned tomorrow? What if Vincent Di Volante does not show up? Or, what if he does show up and there're dead dancers found in the men's rooms? And…and… what if I trip and fall off my heels? Or worse, what if you step on my foot and my ankle twists and breaks like Tavia's? What if it snaps like a twig and makes a loud—"

Nathan gathered her into his arms. "First, things rarely go as planned. You of all people should know that, darlin'. Secondly, I'm more worried that Di Volante will give us the slip, more than he won't be in attendance. I believe where Isadora is…Vincent Di Volante isn't far away. As for you falling on your own? Not a chance. You're way too graceful. You're a fantastic dancer. Nope.

If you fall, I'll have everything to do with it. I just hope you don't get hurt if that should happen. No guarantees, though."

Silja leaned forward. "Tell him what you told me this afternoon, Fiona. You know, about the Stockholm Syndrome stuff."

"Stockholm Syndrome?" Nathan began. "We see that all the time, especially with domestic violence cases. It's amazing how an abused woman will protect the man who abuses her. What were your thoughts on the subject?"

"You mentioned earlier today that when you visit with Isadora it seems like there's another person in the house. And let's face it, not everyone has a ghostly grandma like I do. So, perhaps there is someone in that house, and that person is Vincent Di Volante. Is it possible she's protecting this man for some reason? Or she was forced to protect him at some point, and now it's become a habit—a habit that became a relationship? And if so, why? Why would a beautiful, talented woman like Isadora Danza protect a murderer? You haven't mentioned any signs of physical abuse when you've visited with her—black eyes, bruises of any sort, but there are many ways someone can administer abuse: emotionally, mentally, verbally. Oftentimes, abuse is not accompanied by physical wounds."

Nathan turned toward Silja. "Do ya see? Do ya see why I'm head-over-heels about this girl? She's not just beautiful and talented, but she's become one slick sleuth. You may be right. I think we may very well have a case of Stockholm Syndrome. That said, I'm not exactly sure if Isadora Danza is the abused. Oh, I believe at one time she may have been, but I'm starting to wonder if she had taken on the role of the abuser. I'm bound and determined to find out tomorrow."

"And just how do you plan to that, Detective Landry? Or should I say, Walter Baumbacher?" Fiona inquired.

Nathan chuckled. "No…no need for the alias. Isadora is well aware who I am, so we'll be using our real names."

"What a relief. Now, how do you plan to deal with Vincent and Isadora?"

His lips curled. "Flirting—merciless flirtation."

Fiona's hand went to her chest. "Oh, Nathan, I hope you don't end up dead in the men's room."

Nathan chuckled. "Yeah, me too."

℘ ℘ ℘

It wasn't bad enough Fiona hadn't slept for one second all night, but the mambo dress was itchy beyond belief, and tight, and uncomfortable, and skimpy—way, *wa-a-ay* too skimpy. She pulled and tugged and scratched and winced. Well, at least the awful dress kept her mind off the fact that she was about half-crazy with nerves.

Nathan?

He was as calm as could be. He looked so incredibly handsome in his red silk shirt and tight dance slacks. Unfortunately, they had not bumped into Isadora Danza. So far, Nathan had not had an opportunity to "*flirt mercilessly*" with the dancer. Fiona noticed Officer Wyatt Hayes sitting in the audience. He was sipping a cup of coffee while constantly scanning the crowd. She was most certain other officers were stationed throughout the audience as well. Her gaze met Tavia's—she was lumbering into a seat while trying not to bonk anyone over the head with her crutches. When Tavia reached her seat, she blew her a kiss. Fiona smiled—hopefully, she'd forgiven Nathan. She was certain Tavia would be proud how far he'd come since her broken ankle. Tavia moved her crutches aside to give an old woman room to take the seat next to her.

Fabulous dancers in fabulous costumes were darting about, preparing to perform. The novice division of the mambo competition was first on the roster—at least she'd get her first competition out of the way almost immediately.

The David Lawrence Convention Center in downtown Pittsburgh was packed and bustling with excitement—the Glass Slipper Ballroom Competition was about to begin!

Fiona let out a groan. She wanted nothing more than to rip the scratchy costume from her body. Silja tapped her on the shoulder. "I've got your backpack, so you don't have to worry where you laid it."

"I wish you could take this costume too, so I wouldn't have to worry about how itchy I am," Fiona moaned.

"Suck it up, *Buttercup*," Silja replied.

"I'm sorry you're so uncomfortable, Fiona, because I think you look…wow…just *wow*," Nathan said.

Fiona couldn't suppress the grin that stretched across her face. She glanced at Silja, who tossed her a wink.

"Before we start the competition, we have a special surprise this evening," an announcer's voice rang out throughout the huge area, and everyone stopped to listen. "We are so honored to have the beautiful, Isadora Danza as one of our prestigious judges tonight, and we are thrilled to announce that tonight is Isadora's *seventieth* birthday!" The crowd exploded with applause and whoops. "To celebrate the joy of ballroom dancing at any age, Isadora has chosen a partner to open the Glass Slipper Competition festivities with a saucy tango! Ladies and gentlemen...the fantastic, Isadora Danza dancing with, Chad Quinn!"

Instantly, Fiona stopped tugging at her costume. Her eyes widened and her jaw dropped. Nathan leaned in close. "Did he just say what I thought he just said? He couldn't be talking about your brother, Chad Quinn. It's gotta be some other Chad Qu—"

Just then, a bright white spotlight illuminated the open space between the bleachers where Isadora Danza stood in a royal blue flamenco dress, poised to make a grand entrance. Rhinestones adorned the scooped neckline of the amazing dress. The glass stones glimmered over the velvet bodice while the big full skirt swayed and sheer fabric flowed from armbands as she strutted forward with chin held high into position. Just as dignified, self-confident, and graceful, Isadora was being escorted by...that's right, Fiona's brother, Chad Quinn! With all the grace and elegance of Astaire, he spun Isadora into her beginning pose.

The itchy, tight, uncomfortable costume was all but forgotten—Fiona simply could not believe her eyes. Around a gasp, she exclaimed, "How can this be? Chad never attended a prom. He's never approached a dance floor at a wedding—not even for the chicken dance or the hokey-pokey. I've never seen him so much as tap his toe to music, for crying out loud. When did this come about? And how did he come to be chosen by a top-notch ballroom dancer for this…this…for *this*!"

"Apparently, your brother has another life—a very *interesting* and secret life," Nathan put in. Exchanging glances, Fiona could see he was just as shocked by what he was about to witness as she was. He dug into his pocket to pull out a Snickers—evidently as an event snack.

Silja stepped up to stand behind Fiona and Nathan, she whispered, "Is that your brother, *Chad*? I can't believe it. Why didn't you tell me he danced ballroom? When did he start dancing?"

Nathan replied, "Yes, it is. She can't believe it either, and because she didn't know, lastly, she has absolutely no idea."

Fiona flipped her palm out to Silja. "Cell phone."

Silja fumbled with Fiona's backpack for only a moment before coming up with the phone and placing it in her hand. "What are you gonna do?"

"Mom wanted to know what Chad's been up to. Well, I guess it's time she finds out," Fiona stated as she marched through the din of onlookers for a better position.

"And there it is," Silja said.

Unwrapping the bite-size Snickers, while inspecting the audience, Nathan asked, "There's what?"

"The legendary Quinn sibling rivalry is still very much alive and well. I really don't know why. Chad always wins—*always*."

Nathan tossed the Snickers bar into his mouth. "Don't I know it."

ELEVEN

What on earth was her little brother, Chad, trying to pull? Since when did *he* dance? Since when did he do anything other than watch sports, talk about sports, or attend sporting events? There had to be a woman behind this new interest in the finer arts. Good. Now, she needed to find out who this woman was—if for no other reason than to give her mother hope. Well, at least that's what she was trying to convince herself of for what she was about to do—take a picture and send it off to mom.

Mom would be totally shocked.

Chad would be forced to play a hearty game of twenty questions by nine o'clock this evening.

Mom would be excited beyond belief at the thought of Chad settling down—maybe grandchildren. Maybe, *just maybe*, this would get Mom off her back.

Chad would be sooo mad—he would want to exact revenge.

That was perfectly okay, because it was *her turn* to tell embarrassing stories at Thanksgiving or Christmas dinner—maybe both! She would have to take some time to think of a few.

Fiona had managed to score a prime spot right in front of the horde of spectators when the lights went to blue and the disco ball suspended above the dance floor began to whirl, tossing millions of glittering prisms throughout the hall. The tango music began and Chad and Isadora glided across the floor. Every cell phone in the house was clicking and blinking, including Fiona's. Her brother spun the vivacious veteran dancer around the space as if he'd been dancing for a lifetime and the crowd loved every moment of the dazzling display. Fiona held her cell phone to her chest to watch—he was truly a wonderful dancer.

Chad was elegant…graceful…jubilant. What?

Hey, her brother was good—like, really good!

A tinge of pride washed over her.

She smiled, and before she knew it, the crowd was cheering and applauding as Chad and Isadora took their gracious bows—and that's when Chad's gaze met Fiona's.

Chad's eyes widened. He looked as if he'd just swallowed a squirrel. Giving him a thumbs-up gesture, Fiona smiled brightly while holding up her cell phone. Yeah, she was proud of little brother, but she wanted him to know she had the goods on him.

Evil?

Maybe a little, but she had so few evil moments— she needed to savor every second.

Chad took a step toward Fiona only to have Isadora tug him back and plant a huge kiss on his lips. The kiss was deep and long—too long in Fiona's opinion. She blinked back, and she noticed her brother was taken aback by the kiss and its length too. When Isadora finally let go of the embrace, she strutted toward the crowd where Nathan greeted her. Again, Fiona found herself blinking back. Her detective didn't waste a moment, he put his plan into motion, and she was rather shocked by how aggressively her Nathan could flirt.

Yikes.

Isadora didn't appear to be affronted by his advances, rather, she welcomed them. She immediately took Nathan into her arms and kissed him as passionately as she had kissed Chad. Fiona searched the throng for Silja to find her with her hand cupped over her mouth. Just then, she felt someone jabbing her right shoulder. She turned to come face to face with her younger brother.

Chad's face was brilliant red—not from exertion, but rather, annoyance. "What are you doing here?" That's when he noticed her costume. "You're *competing*?"

Fiona pitched him an ornery grin. "Sure am. Ya know, just the other day I was talking with mom, and she asked if I'd seen you lately. She was wondering what you've been up to. Now, I don't have to tell her—" She held up her cell phone. "I can *show* her."

"Happy birthday, Isadora!" the announcer boomed. "At seventy, she's still got it! Wooing audiences with her moves and men with her beauty and charm."

Once again, Chad's eyes grew wide. "Isn't that your *boyfriend*?"

Fiona turned to see Nathan twirl Isadora around, bend her backward and kiss her. Double yikes—he was better at this flirting thing than she could have ever imagined! While her attention was zoomed in on Nathan, her brother snatched the cell from her hand. She spun around, grappling for her phone, but before she could grab it from his hand, Chad rushed into the mass of people, holding the phone over his head like a trophy.

Well played, little brother, well played.

"C'mon, Fiona, I want to put the finishing touches on your makeup," Silja called from behind her. Fiona glanced back at Nathan. Yep, he was still "*flirting mercilessly*" with Isadora who was eating up the younger man's attention. Fiona could not quell the spade of jealousy digging into her gut. Silja took her by the arm. "He's pretty good at that, isn't he?"

"Yeah, he never flirts with *me* like that."

Digging through Fiona's backpack, Silja chuckled. "You're a kindergarten teacher."

"Don't remind me."

"We'll give Isadora a few minutes to change and we'll begin the competition with the novice division of Mambo—competitors, please be ready!" the announcer said.

Nathan made his way through the crowd to join Fiona and Silja. While pressing at something inside his left ear, he pulled something from inside his shirt. He studied what looked to be a photograph for a moment, then scanned the crowd.

Fiona peeked over his shoulder. Indeed, he had an old black and white photograph of a man. "Who's that?"

"That is Vincent Di Volante. This is the only photo we could come up with, so I'm gonna have to try to identify him as much older than in this photo—not easy." He shoved the picture back into its place.

Fiona looked over the throng of people. "See any prospects?"

Nathan let out a sigh. "I've seen quite a few who look like this photo. I just have to hope he saw me with Isadora, and he's not happy about it. Well, are you ready?"

"I suppose. So, speaking of Isadora, do *you* think the *seventy-year-old* dancer has still *got it*," Fiona snapped. She bit her lip. She didn't mean to snap, but there it was again, a big old snap.

Nathan blinked back. "Got what?"

"*It*—whatever *it* is. Sex appeal, beauty, talent—you know, *it*."

"Aw, c'mon, Fiona. I told you I have to flirt with her—it's the only way I'm gonna draw Vincent Di Volante out into the open—where I need him to be. She's a seventy-year-old woman, for cryin' out loud. Yeah, she's still got *it*—for a seventy-year-old. Let's just hope Vincent thinks so too."

Fiona felt ashamed. "I know, I know. I'm just nervous. I'm sorry. I guess I'm sort of wishing you'd flirt with me that way."

He jabbed his thumb over his shoulder. "Like that? Like I just did with Isadora?"

She shot him a sheepish look. "Yeah, like that."

Nathan raised his eyebrows, then furrowed them. "Hm."

"Hey, don't forget to give me your cell phone. You don't want to go out on the dance floor with it." With a baffled look, Silja searched Fiona's person. "Where'd you stuff it, anyway?"

Fiona let out a huff. "Oh, don't worry, we'll get it back—after Chad's had his way with it."

Silja and Nathan exchanged smirks. Rolling her eyes in self-reprimand, Fiona shook her head. "I should know better than to mess with him—he's so much more cunning than I am."

"*Everybody's* more cunning than you are, Fiona. Hey, don't look now," Silja began as she handed a pair of sunglasses to Nathan. "Your brother and his partner are lined up for the Novice Mambo Division."

Fiona craned her neck to see over the crowd. "Wait a minute—isn't that Miss Angela? The Miss Angela from your ill-fated ballroom dance classes?"

"Sure looks like her." Nathan dropped a pair of aviator sunglasses over his eyes and took Fiona by the hand. "It's go time, darlin'."

"Listen, Chad may be more cunning than I am, but he's not going to beat me at something I've been doing all my life. Now, let's get out there and kick some ballroom butt, Landry." Fiona squeezed Nathan's hand and dragged him toward the line.

Nathan looked back at Silja. "Uh, oh."

TWELVE

Silja could hardly contain her excitement. She felt she was almost as nervous as Fiona, although Fiona appeared to have a new sense of confidence, or maybe it was blatant determination, when she and Nathan stepped into line to wait for the call to the dance floor. Pushing and slipping through the crowd of onlookers, Silja managed to get a good spot to view the competition. She glanced over to the line of competitors who were about to compete in the novice division of Mambo Dance only to find there were a mere three couples in the lineup; Chad and Nathan's former dance instructor, Angela, a rather old-looking couple who appeared to be around seventy or so, and at the end of the short line, Fiona and Nathan. Silja caught Fiona's gaze and waved at her.

"I see you have someone in this division," a middle-aged man who was standing next to her said.

"Yes, my friend and her boyfriend are competing for the first time. I used to compete, so I helped them with their routine," Silja explained.

The man pointed to the elderly couple who were standing in front of Fiona and Nathan. "That's my dad and his new wife, Thelma. This is their first time too. Of course, they don't think they'll win, but they've been having so much fun learning. I think it's just great."

"Oh, my, that is wonderful. How long have they been married?"

"About six months. Thelma has macular degeneration—she's legally blind, and dad is dancing on two replaced knees, but hey, they're cuttin' the rug anyway."

"God bless them. I hope they do well," Silja replied.

Just then, the judges took their places at the tables and bright lights illuminated the dance floor. The announcer boomed, "And now ladies and gentlemen, we will begin the Glass Slipper Ballroom Competition with the Novice Mambo Division. Dancers, please take your places on the floor as I call out your names. Our first couple, Angela Rivetti and Chad Quinn."

Chad and Angela trotted across the dance floor until they found a satisfactory spot—directly in front of the judges' table. Chad spun his dark-haired partner and they stepped into a pose.

"Our second couple, Robert and Thelma Wainwright. Like our beloved Isadora, this older couple is living proof that ballroom dancing is ageless!"

The audience clapped and cheered as the elderly couple made their way onto the floor. Their entrance was not nearly as graceful as Chad and Angela's. Robert was very careful to lead Thelma to their position. Silja felt a pinch of sorrow for the old couple—they didn't stand a chance against the younger more agile couples in the competition. The man standing next to her whistled loudly for his father and stepmother.

"And now our final couple will take a place on the dance floor—Fiona Quinn and Nathan Landry."

Fiona and Nathan trotted to a spot near Chad and Angela. Nathan spun Fiona, dipped her, and then they struck a pose.

"That's all of them! Ladies and gentlemen, please welcome our dancers for the Novice Division of Mambo to the dance floor!"

The great space erupted with applause and cheers. Slowly the ovation fell away and a mambo beat filled the convention center. Hips swaying and arms moving in mambo style, Fiona approached Nathan to whip the sunglasses from his face and toss them to the floor. Nathan spun in place and then grabbed Fiona by the waist.

Silja grabbed the arm of the man standing next to her. "I just love that part!"

"Yes, it was quite good, but aren't you afraid they'll step on or trip over the glasses?"

"Um…hope not."

Fiona and Nathan went to a closed position to perform an open box step when Chad whirled Angela around to plow into Fiona who lost her footing to fall against Nathan! Angela tossed them a smart smirk as she shimmied her way toward Chad who fell to one knee for her to twirl around and drop into a backbend across it.

Uh, oh, not good, Silja thought.

She saw that look on Fiona's face—the one she used to get when Chad had pushed her a little too far. She had a reeling feeling the competition was going to take an ugly turn—it was going to transform from dance competition into a battle zone!

"That wasn't supposed to happen, was it?" the man asked.

"No. I don't know what that was about," Silja said.

She could see Nathan trying to reason with Fiona, but it was of little use, she was hot. No one could get under Fiona's skin like her little brother. Silja had no doubt the next move would not be pretty. The next set in the choreography was a traveling move to the left, directly toward Chad and Angela. Nathan was taking smaller steps than the choreography called for. God bless him, he was making every attempt to diffuse the situation to no avail. Pulling Nathan along, Fiona strutted across the floor with relentless purpose.

Well, at least she's in step with the music.

Silja cupped her right hand over her mouth, while involuntarily she'd wrapped the fingers of her left around the poor man's arm so tightly he yelped, "Ouch!"

She winced.

She grimaced.

She flinched.

And yes, there were moments she had to turn her face away because she could no longer bear to watch. Finally, she chanced a peek at what was taking place when, around his discomfort, the man managed to ask, "What are they doing now?"

"God, I wish I knew," Silja moaned. She glanced over to the judges who were watching the disastrous dance debacle with dazed expressions. Isadora sat back in her seat with her hands on her chest.

Chad and Angela had paused into a pose. Fiona popped her hip to slam into Chad—hard! The couple toppled toward the floor, but before they made purchase with the cement, Chad managed to grab Fiona's hand and that's when her toe stepped on the sunglasses she'd tossed to the floor. Slipping on the glasses, her legs came out from under her to slog forward.

Nathan stumbled forward.

He grappled for Fiona's arm.

He couldn't grab hold.

His efforts were in vain—Fiona fell to the floor on top of Chad and Angela.

The audience laughed and pointed.

Nathan was the only man left standing. Well, except for the elderly couple who were not just cutting the rug with their mambo skills—they were shredding it to pieces! At this point, the judges had directed their attention to the older couple. When the music came to a halt, the judges' passed their cards down the row at lightning speed to the steward who collected them at the end of the table.

"For obvious reasons," the announcer began. "There will be no second or third place prizes awarded in this division. Now, ladies and gentlemen please give a rousing applause to our first-place winners, Robert and Thelma Wainwright! Congratulations!"

The man standing next to Silja hurried through the crowd toward his parents.

ભ ભ ભ

Nathan took Fiona by the hand to yank her to her feet. "Seriously, Fiona? I can't believe it. I've never seen you behave like that."

"You've never been around when Chad just… he just…ugh!" Her hands drawn into tight fists, she marched off the dance floor into the crowd.

Nathan offered a hand to Angela. She shot him a severe look. "Well! Looks like you actually made it to a competition, Walter! And looks like we got the exact result I warned you about!"

"*Walter*?" Chad jeered. "His name isn't *Walter*. His name is Nathan—as in Detective Nathan Landry."

"Well, I hope he's better at being a cop than he is a dancer—but I doubt it! Don't call me, Chad!" She turned to stomp off the dance floor.

Chad took several steps after her but a man in a dark suit stepped in front of him. His voice was deep and laced with an Italian accent. "You two gentlemen need to come with me."

Nathan locked eyes with the man. He appeared to be up in years, yet fit and robust for his age which Nathan figured to be about seventy-two. Yeah, he looked like he could be, Vincent Di Volante.

"Oh, great, the ballroom competition police are here. I'll be with ya in a minute, buddy. I gotta talk to Angela before she—"

The man pressed the pocket of his suit jacket forward—it was most obvious the business end of a pistol was pointed at them. Chad took a step backward, bumping into Nathan. Hitching his chin, the older man glowered at Nathan. "C'mon, you too, Romeo."

Nathan glanced over at Isadora. She was involved in a conversation with several of the judges. The couples lined up for the next round stepped aside to give the three men passage.

The announcer said, "We're ready for our next group of dancers for the Intermediate Mambo Division. Dancers, please step onto the dance floor when your names are called!"

~ ~ ~

"Fiona!" Tavia called over the music—the second round of the Mambo competition had begun.

Fiona turned to see Tavia hopping toward her on crutches with an aged woman following closely behind. The woman, who walked with a cane, was sophisticated-looking. The woman was on the short side. She wore a grey suit with a grey and pink floral scarf tucked into the breast. She appeared to be in her mid-seventies or perhaps early-eighties.

Catching up with her friend, Tavia said, "Well, it was pretty good until the end. I couldn't believe that other couple, and then I couldn't believe *your* reaction." She snorted. "I've never seen that side of you, Fiona. Wow. You were like the *boss*, well, until you slipped on the glasses. What was going on out there?"

Fiona could feel the heated flush rising from her throat to her face.

He'd done it again.

She'd let him do it.

Fact was, no one, absolutely no one could get under her skin or make her head explode like her little brother.

As per usual, she'd allowed Chad to get the best of her—this time had to be the worst.

Around a haggard sigh, Fiona managed, "Yeah, more than I expected. Is there something I can help you with? I'd really like to get out of this costume, and try to calm down before the next hot mess begins."

"I need to talk with Nate. This is Vincent Di Volante's older sister, Maria Francesco," Tavia explained. "She was sitting with me, and she saw her brother leave with Nate and the guy who had the same last name as you, do you know him? Do you know where they went?"

Fiona let out a gasp. "Oh, my God. I hope they didn't go to the men's room!"

THIRTEEN

Vincent directed Nathan and Chad down a long closed-off corridor. "This way." He glanced furtively over his shoulder, then pulled the gun from his pocket. The hallway was dimly lit. Their footsteps echoed through the wide empty space. The Mambo music drifting from the competition was nothing more than a faraway whisper.

"It's driving me about crazy, so I gotta ask, what are you doing here, Chad? C'mon, ballroom dancing is completely out of character for you," Nathan said.

Chad's panicked gaze shifted from Vincent to Nathan. "I let Angela talk me into taking ballroom classes—and this is what it got me."

"Yeah, women can make ya do the darnedest things, can't they? So, where are we going, Mr. Di Volante? To the men's room?" Nathan asked.

Sweat saturated Chad's forehead. His face was flushed and his eyes were wide with trepidation. "Why would we go to the men's room? Hey look, I know we totally messed up the novice division, but I don't think we deserve to be shot for it. Let's face it, dude, my sister got a little carried away. Okay, okay, I egged her on. I always do—it's expected of me. I stole her cell phone from her to delete the pictures she took of me dancing. In my defense, she was gonna send those pictures to my mother. Do you have any idea what I would have been put through when my mom saw those pictures? She would've asked question after question. Nag, nag, nag. Who is that woman in the picture? Are you dating her? Is it serious? We didn't know you liked *older* women—like *super* older women. When did you start dancing? She would've gone on and on."

"Wow. It's just like having Fiona in the room," Nathan remarked.

"Hey!" Chad pointed a warning finger at Nathan. "I'm *nothing* like Fiona."

"Oh, yes you are."

"Am not."

Nathan snorted. "Are too."

"I. Am. *Not.*"

"Indeed, you *are*," Nathan said.

Wearing a surly expression, Vincent stared at the two men. "Why would Isadora choose *him* to dance with her? What is your relationship with my Isadora? Yes, she is older, but she is still as beautiful as ever."

Chad held his hands up in surrender. "Look, dude, I was told she picked me to do the intro number. I don't know why. Angela said she was a famous ballroom dancer, but that's all I know. Is that what this is about? You think there's something between me and Isadora Danza?

She's like fifty-years older than me, man. Nathan, *do* something." He lowered his voice. "Can't you contact your *people* or something?"

Shaking his head, Nathan shrugged. "You can never find a cop when you need one."

"You won't be making jokes for long, Detective Landry. You come to my home to win Isadora's heart, and then you come to the Glass Slipper to make your play. Did you think I would stand by and let you take my Isadora?" Vincent said. They arrived at a door marked, *men's room*. He hitched his chin toward the restroom door.

"Others have tried to take Isadora, haven't they?" Nathan pulled the door open and stepped inside. The lights came on automatically. "Tell me, Mr. Di Volante, how did you do it all these years? How did you manage to keep the fact you were alive from literally everyone? And how did you get Isadora to hide you for all these years—especially after you killed those dancers?"

Chad plopped against one of the sinks along the wall. "This guy is a *murderer*? Great, just great. I work hard to steer clear of this kind of stuff and now you've got me right in the middle of one of your murder things?" He ran a harried hand through his hair. "Not cool, man, not cool—this is Fiona's sort of thing, *not mine*."

"Those *dancers* were just like *you*. They wanted my Isadora for their own. But she was promised to *me*. Our parents had made an agreement. I'd been pa-tient long enough, she'd evaded our parents' wishes for long enough. It was time she gave up this man she was involved with and do what was expected of her. I told her I would not harm him if she let him go," Vincent bit out.

"What man?" Nathan inquired.

"I don't know his name. I never did, and I don't care to know it now."

"The man who occupied your grave for forty years?"

Vincent cocked his head to the side for a moment. "Forty-*three* years."

"I stand corrected, forty-*three* years," Nathan replied. He pointed to his pocket to signal that he was getting something. Slowly, he retrieved several bite-size candies. He held the candy out. "Snickers, anyone? They're really nice for a little pick-me-up."

Ninja-quick, Vincent plucked one from his hand and stuffed it into his pocket. "For later."

His expression brighter, Chad pushed off the sink he was leaning against. "Oh! I get it now! This is payback! This is a ruse orchestrated by my big sister to get back at me for…for whatever she thinks she needs to get back at me for. Lord knows, the list is crazy long. I like it. This is good. It's really good, but, I'm not falling for it, Nate."

Vincent let out a beleaguered breath. "How do I get him to shut up?"

Not lifting his gaze while fumbling with the candy wrapper, Nathan lifted a shoulder. "You'll have to shoot him."

Vincent raised the gun to take aim.

Stepping back, Chad's eyes popped wider. His jaw dropped open.

"Vincent Di Volante! I cannot believe what a vile thing you and Isabella have done!" A woman yelled out.

Her Italian accent bounced and echoed throughout the restroom.

Stunned by the sound of his sister's voice, Vincent spun around. "Maria!"

Ditching the candy, Nathan seized the opportunity. He leapt forward to shove Vincent to the floor, wrestling the gun from Vincent's hand while pinning his arms to the cement. Still, the older man squirmed to find his freedom.

A man's voice rang out, "Stay down, Di Volante, you're under arrest!"

Expelling a grunt, Vincent stilled. Nathan looked up at Officer Wyatt Hays who had his revolver trained on Vincent. "Thanks for showing up, Wyatt."

"Eh, all in a day's work," Wyatt said. He handed Nathan a pair of handcuffs.

"You were gonna let him shoot me. You *suggested* that he shoot me," Chad said.

"I wasn't gonna let him shoot you. You're Fiona's brother, for cryin' out loud," Nathan replied as he pushed to his feet and helped Wyatt pull Vincent from the floor. Wyatt began to recite the Miranda Rights to Vincent as he escorted him past Maria and out of the men's room.

"You knew Wyatt was coming?" Chad asked. Nathan nodded. "How?"

Nathan dug into his left ear to pull out a tiny earbud. "I was on it."

"Why didn't you give me some kind of signal that everything was cool?"

"And ruin all the fun? No way." He turned toward Maria. "Hello, Mrs. Francesco, I'm Detective Landry, we spoke on the phone. I'm surprised to see you here." The woman looked bewildered by the excitement, and sorrowful to see her brother hauled away. Nathan offered her his arm. Favoring him with a withered smile, she took his arm as Chad followed along. They made their way out of the men's room into a now busy corridor.

"When you told me that my brother was still alive, how could I not come? And when my granddaughter found this competition on the internet, and Isabella was a judge, I had plane tickets for Pittsburgh within five minutes." Maria and Nathan could see Isadora standing with Tavia farther down the corridor. She was wearing handcuffs. Raising her chin to a haughty level, she completely ignored Vincent's pleading expression as Wyatt led him past her. "Officer Andrews told me Vincent will be charged with the murder of those three men, and possibly one more. But I must ask, will Isabella be charged as well or will she go free?"

As they drew closer to Isadora, Nathan met her intense gaze. "I'm sure charges will be brought up against her, if nothing else, harboring a criminal for all those years. We'll see."

An officer approached Nathan. He held up a clipboard for the detective to see. Nathan turned to Maria. "It was nice to meet you, Mrs. Francesco. Although, I wish it were better circumstances. Thank you for all your help, and I know it is of little comfort, but I'm sorry for the years of pain you must've endured. Could you please go with this officer? He'd like to take a statement. You too, Chad."

While Maria and Chad followed the officer off to the side, Nathan made his way toward Isadora.

Isadora favored him with a svelte smile. "My dear handsome, Nathan. When did you know?"

"The day Detective Yallowitz and I visited your home. I knew you were hiding something very important by something you said," Nathan supplied.

"That was over a week ago, Nathan." He could see her searching her memory to recollect the conversation from that particular afternoon. "I can't imagine what I could've said—"

"You brought your cat into the house and whispered into her ear, *dobbiamo stare attenti ora, amore mio*—we must be careful now, my love."

Isadora blinked back, her mouth dropped open just a bit, and then just as quickly, she reconciled with her composure. "Molto bene, Detective. I had no idea you spoke Italian."

"I spent two summers in Sicily when I was a teen on an exchange program. I had to learn the language because the family I was staying with refused to acknowledge me if I didn't speak in Italian. At first, I was put off, but now in my profession, I know they've done me a great service," Nathan explained.

"I was forced to take him in. I was forced to protect him," Isadora said with a whimper in her voice.

"I'm sure you were—until you weren't. Now, I must ask you a vital question, and please be aware your answer will give another family closure."

"What is it you want to know?"

"Who occupied Vincent Di Volante's grave for all those years?" Nathan asked. Isadora's gaze fell to the floor. "I know you know, Isadora. I've seen video footage of you placing flowers on the grave. Who is he? Was he the man Vincent promised to spare if you gave him up? And is that why he was in the house the night the police showed up to arrest Vincent?"

"Say nothing, Isadora," a man called out from behind. He rushed to Isadora's side. "One of the judges called to tell me about this terrible mess. I'm Harvey Berg, Isadora has nothing to say until I've been fully informed of the charges against her, and I've had a chance to speak with my client."

Nathan raised his hands in surrender then turned to make his way toward Fiona and Silja who were waiting where someone had strung police tape across the corridor to keep people out of the area. As he ducked under the tape, he smiled at Fiona. "Well, looks like Isadora is in very good hands. If anyone can prove she suffered from Stockholm Syndrome for forty years, Harvey Berg can. Hey, you're dressed in your regular clothes."

He was right. Fiona had changed into a pair of jeans and a Kennywood Amusement Park T-shirt. "Well, under the circumstances, I didn't see a reason to put on the waltz dress."

"Are you kidding? And waste all that time and sweat and practice we put Silja through—not to mention ourselves? Besides, I was looking forward to seeing you in that dress." He took Fiona by the hand, twirled her in a circle, dipped her backward, and kissed her passionately. "Is that how you wanted me to kiss you, Ms. Quinn?"

Fiona blinked back. Dazed but totally enthralled, she sighed, "Yeah, Detective Landry, just like *that*."

"Good. Now, get in there and get dressed so we can kick some ballroom butt." He pulled her to an upright position.

Fiona tossed her head back in laughter. "I'm on it!"

Pulling her close, Nathan pressed his forehead against hers. "I don't know a whole lot about dancing, but I know one thing for sure—you've definitely got *it*."

"Okay, you two, we don't have a lot of time until they call for the Novice Waltz Division dancers to line up. And I have a long drive back to Harverton when this competition is over. So, let's go, Quinn," Silja said. The two girls hurried away to get ready.

Someone tapped Nathan on the shoulder. He turned to find Tavia Andrews. She said, "Remember that list you asked me to look for? The men at Angelo Moretti's house playing cards the night Vincent Di Volante supposedly died?"

"It's a little late now, Tav."

She handed him the list. "Better late than never, luv."

"You've got them all marked as deceased, except for one who's in an Alzheimer's unit."

"Yeah, the list was useless. Anyway, remember the research you asked me to do on Lucille Stacy-Smith? Well, I've found her youngest daughter, Blanche. Lucille had just given birth to her before she was institutionalized in Dixmont. Blanche is in her forties, and she lives in Sacramento, California. I've got a phone number, and I also know where Edward Smith is too." She handed him a piece of paper.

Nathan took a moment to examine the report she'd given him. "Wow. I think I've been totally blindsided."

Hopping away on her crutches, she called over her shoulder, "If it makes you feel any better, you looked pretty good out there, Landry. I was impressed."

Nathan smiled.

FOURTEEN

Dusk was giving way to nightfall by the time Fiona and Nathan were able to drive home. While hugging a trophy shaped like a glass slipper to her chest, Fiona giggled gleefully as Nathan rolled her Mini Cooper to a stop in front of her house. Sliding from the car, Nathan inquired, "What are you gonna do with that thing, anyway?"

"I'm going to proudly display it in the living room. We won first place at a ballroom dance competition—it's a forever memory." Fiona slipped out of the passenger seat and took Nathan's hand to stroll toward the house.

Nathan rolled his eyes. "We were the only ones in the division. Chad and his partner didn't show up, and that old couple didn't participate. We kind of won by default."

"Hey, we danced beautifully. We didn't forget one step. We were in time with the music. And we did not fall over each other or anyone else. We were not disqualified, therefore, we won fair and square. Silja said she was proud of us before she left," Fiona firmly stated. They made their way up the steps and across the porch. They could hear Harriet barking from inside the house.

"Chad give you back your cell phone?" Nathan asked.

"Yep."

"Are the pictures still on it?"

"Yep."

"That's a shocker. On the other hand, he was pretty shook-up. Maybe he forgot to get rid of them. So, are you gonna send them to your mom?"

Fiona's lips curled.

"Ya know, for a kindergarten teacher, you can be surprisingly wicked," Nathan pointed out.

Around a chuckle, Fiona began to dig through her backpack for her house keys. "And don't you forget it, Detective Landry."

"Duly noted, Ms. Quinn."

The porch light flicked on.

Nathan favored Fiona with a questioning look. She replied with a grin and a nod. Yep, Grandma Ev had turned the light on to help her locate her keys.

"I suppose Grandma Ev knows when your home with all the racket Harriet makes," Nathan suggested.

"Most likely." Fiona opened the door then bent down to let Harriet out of her crate while Nathan held the door open for the little dog. She darted off the porch, did her thing, and then scampered back into the house. Nathan scooped her up to scrub his fingers over her ears.

"Fiona…I know you're tired, and so am I, but before I leave, do you mind if we go upstairs to Ev's apartment. I've got something to tell her."

Fiona searched his face. She could see he was serious and whatever he needed to tell her ghostly grandma was serious as well. "Certainly, let's go."

She took him by the hand and they climbed the main staircase, crossed the second-floor foyer, then stepped into the enclosed stairwell that led to the attic apartment. When they reached the top floor, Nathan set Harriet on the floor. The little dog did not hesitate to enter the apartment space, as she had the last time they visited; likewise, the room wasn't frigid as it had been before.

Nathan approached the small living room area and pulled the sheet from the couch. He gestured for Fiona to have a seat. Harriet jumped up to sidle up next to her mistress, and Nathan made himself comfortable as well.

"What's this all about, Nathan?" Fiona asked.

"A promise I made to your grandma the other day."

"When you told Silja and I to go downstairs and you remained here in the apartment?"

"That's right. I got the coroner's report back—Tavia gave it to me this afternoon and I read it while you and Silja were getting ready for the waltz competition. She also gave me a phone number—I'll get to that in a minute. Fact is, we have the identity of the man who was in the grave who they thought was Vincent Di Volante," Nathan explained while he pulled his cell phone and a note from his pocket. Keeping his eyes on the note, he began to dial.

"Oh, how sad. Yes, it's good that he has finally been identified correctly, but now you have to inform his family that their missing loved one is, in fact, dead," Fiona said.

Nathan took in a braced breath. "That's what I'm doing right now."

"Here? In Grandma's apartment? Don't you usually do that in the office?"

"Not this time." Nathan pressed the speaker button on his phone then set it down face-up on the coffee table.

The phone on the other end was ringing.

"Can you at least tell me who you're calling?"

"Blanche Smith-Munley—Aunt Lucille's youngest child. Turns out, the man who has been in Vincent Di Volante's grave all these years was, Edward Smith—your great-aunt Lucille's husband."

Fiona sat straight up. "Wait—what?"

There was a loud *click*, and then a woman's voice filtered through the phone. "Hello…"

"Hello, Mrs. Blanche Munley? I'm Detective Nathan Landry with the Pittsburgh Homicide Unit."

There was a long pause. Fiona could feel the woman's apprehension wafting through the connection. Finally, she replied, "Yes…this is Blanche Munley, what can I do for you, Detective?"

"I'm calling with some long overdue information about your father, Edward Smith."

There was a moment of hesitation. Blanche managed, "My father? I never knew my father, Detective. Evidentially, he ran away with another woman right after I was born. At least that's the impression my aunt who was raising me came to when he never returned to visit or claim his children. My mother accused him of such behavior, but no one would believe her. She ended up in an institution and died there. By the time I became a teenager, I suppose my aunt gave up the notion that he would come back, and she accepted my mother's accusations. Unfortunately, it was too late for my mother. I certainly hope you're not calling because he's sick or ill or needs money for bail because I'm not interested."

"No, ma'am, and I wouldn't blame you. Fact is, your father is deceased and has been since 1976. Problem is, he's been in a grave marked Vincent Di Volante until about a week ago."

Blanche let out a gasp. "You mean, he's been dead all this time and we thought he'd run away with another woman? Wait a minute. You said you were from the *homicide* unit. Was he murdered?"

Nathan exchanged glances with Fiona. She could see in his eyes the next part of the story was going to be tough.

"No, ma'am, your father was not murdered, but your mother, Lucille, wasn't wrong. Edward Smith was involved with another woman, Isadora Danza. Problem was, Isadora had been promised to a man named, Vincent Di Volante—who was wanted for the murders of three men he believed had been involved with Isadora. Anyway, Vincent told Isadora that he would spare Edward's life if she broke it off with your father and married him. Isadora agreed. She invited Edward to her brother's friend's home one night during a card game. I guess she figured they'd be safer with all those witnesses. She took Edward upstairs to break off their relationship, and that's when Vincent showed up. He was on his way upstairs, unfortunately for Edward, that's when the police showed up too. Isadora thought Vincent was going to kill Edward. She pushed your father out the window, and in the confusion of Vincent's threat and the police yelling, your father managed to jump into Vincent's running car and take off."

Blanche's voice was terse when she said, "Let me guess, the police assumed it was Vincent in the car and shot my father."

"Not exactly. The police chased the car for several blocks. You know how the streets in Pittsburgh can be—lots of steep hills and lots of turns. Your father didn't maneuver one of the bends. He crashed, and the car went up in flames. The driver was burned beyond recognition, and yes, the police assumed it was Vincent Di Volante. That's how your father came to be buried in his grave for all these years."

Blanche asked, "And this Vincent Di Volante? What became of him?"

"We've apprehended him. He's being brought up on a list of charges."

A whimper wafted through the connection. "All these years we thought my father had run away with another woman, and maybe he was going to, but maybe, he had intentions of breaking it off with that woman. We'll never know the truth. My father never got the chance to make that decision, but this Vincent fellow murdered three people and was able to live his life while my father lay in his grave."

"I'm so very sorry, Mrs. Munley. I know this has been a lot to absorb, and you may need time to think, but the coroner needs to know what you'd like done with Mr.

Smith's remains. He can have them shipped to you or you may want to bury them next to your mother."

She sniffled. "You're right, Detective. This is a lot to absorb, and yes, I need to think, and I need to talk with my family. My brothers are gone, but I will talk this over with my husband and my daughters. Can I contact you when I've thought this through? I know time is of the essence."

"Of course. You can contact me at this number. And, Mrs. Munley…I'm very acquainted with cousins you've probably never met. They are wonderful people. I think you may want to get to know them."

Her voice cracked. "I think I would like that very much, Detective. I will most likely be in Pittsburgh soon to take care of my father's arrangements. May I contact you then, and perhaps you can arrange for me to meet them?"

"I'd be happy to, Mrs. Munley, and I know they'd be thrilled to meet you as well. Thank you."

"No, thank *you*, Detective." With that, the line went dead.

Nathan turned toward Fiona who was shaking her head. "What a story. Mom said Edward just seemingly disappeared, and now we know why. I feel so bad for Blanche and her brothers. They thought terrible things about their father for all these years. I mostly feel bad for Lucille. They thought Lucille had lost her mind so they put her in Dixmont, and she was right all the time— Edward *was* having an affair, with Isadora Danza. On top of it all, she was most likely suffering from *postpartum* depression—Lucille was terribly misunderstood."

"That's for sure," Nathan put in.

Fiona leaned back against the couch. "But, I don't get it. Why didn't Isadora simply tell the police the truth? Why did she agree to hide Vincent all these years?"

"According to Harvey Berg, Isadora claims Vincent threatened to tell the police she knew all about the murders of the dancers. He told her that he would expose her as an accomplice, and she would spend years in prison too. And, according to Berg, Isadora believed him. She was terrified. So, she protected him. They lived together and traveled the world together for many years. As a matter of fact, they left the country immediately after Edward's death and didn't return for several years. As we suspected, Berg is going for a Stockholm Syndrome defense. Knowing Harvey Berg, he'll get her acquitted on that very defense."

"But Vincent won't go free, right?"

"Oh, no. I think Vincent will spend the rest of his life in prison." Nathan took a piece of paper from his jacket, pushed up from the couch, and made his way over to Grandma Ev's desk. He opened the middle drawer, laid the paper inside, and then closed it.

"What was that?" Fiona asked.

"The coroner's report—in case Ev wants to look it over."

"Ya know what? I'm feeling a sense of calm falling over Gram's apartment. I'm feeling like Lucille has forgiven my grandma for the non-communication, and I think Gram is feeling better too."

"Funny, I'm kind of getting the same sensations," Nathan said. He shook his head as if he were shocked at the feelings he was experiencing, then hitching his chin toward the analog TV on the stand near the couch, he asked, "Hey, does that old TV still work?"

"Oh, goodness, no. Well, I'm sure it will turn on, but it's not connected to my cable or internet service. The poor thing has just been sitting up here on its stand for many years. But it does have a VCR hooked up to it, and Grandma had some great old movies," Fiona supplied. "Have you ever seen *Gone with the Wind* or *Casablanca*?"

"I've never seen *Gone with the Wind*. I know it's a pretty long movie, and it's pretty late—"

Fiona pushed away from the couch to rummage through the pile of VCR tapes on the lower shelf of the TV stand. "No worries, it's Saturday night and we're both off tomorrow—let's watch it." She pressed the "on" button. Indeed, the TV came on, but only snowy figures filled the screen. She pushed a tape into the VCR and the screen announced a warning about showing the film in a public place without permission.

Nathan flattened his hands and pushed against the cushions on the couch. "The couch seems comfortable enough. Okay, I'm game, if you are."

"I sure am. I used to love watching TV up here with Gram. The movie's about to get started, can you get the light, Nathan?" Fiona asked.

Letting out a sigh, he looked at the light switch on the wall at the top of the stairs. "I'll *try*." He made his way across the room, then swatted the switch to the off position. He waited. The lights remained off. Shrugging, he returned to the couch while pulling a bite-size Snickers from his pocket.

With wide eyes, Fiona turned toward Nathan. "Hey! The lights stayed out. See? Grandma *totally* approves of you."

Unwrapping the candy, Nathan glanced toward the switch. With a not so convincing tone, he said, "Yeah… how about that?"

Fiona cocked her head to the side. "What's wrong?"

"I dunno. I'm thinking I might'a liked it the other way. You know, when she used to toy with my patience." While the opening scene to *Gone with the Wind* began to play, Nathan cuddled Fiona into his arms. "Um, Fiona… what if I kissed you passionately like I did earlier?"

"Mmmm, you can kiss me like that *anytime*."

Suddenly, the lights came on.

Fiona pushed back from Nathan's embrace, laughing.

Tossing the Snickers into his mouth, Nathan said, "Now, that's more like it."

The End

A NOTE FROM C.S. MCDONALD...

MY SEARCH FOR THE
ENIGMATIC LUCILLE SMITH

"How you feel about your family is a complicated thing." This is my favorite line from the movie, *Home Alone*. I find the line to be one of the most honest lines delivered in a movie. No matter who you are, or how close or alienated you may be with your family, I believe this line to be absolutely spot on. Lord knows, Fiona's relationship with her brother, Chad, is certainly a complicated thing. As the author, and you the reader, we find Fiona and Chad's rapport humorous, but for our dear Fiona, it is indeed complicated.

I find it most intriguing that no matter how you feel about your family, at some point in time, it seems, everybody becomes interested in finding out more about their family history. I think the urge to know more about your roots happens later in life when life slows down—the kids are grown, perhaps you've retired, or like me, someone in your family tree sparks a curiosity.

To be honest, since I began writing the Fiona Quinn Mysteries in 2016 and since making the decision to use my grandmother, Evelyn Burrell, as one of the characters, I find myself with renewed interest in my family origins where there once was absolutely none.

Other than my grandmother, I've included Wilbur Stacy as a character in book number two, *Merry Murder*. In that story, Wilbur played the role of Santa at the local mall and ended up being murdered. So, was Wilbur Stacy a real person, a member of my family tree, and most importantly, was he murdered?

Yes, yes, and…well, no.

Wilbur was my grandmother's older brother. My grandmother had nine siblings. Wilbur was the second to the oldest of the group and was *eighteen* years my grandmother's senior. From my research, Wilbur led a fairly "regular" life. He was never married. He worked in the mill, and he died at the age of seventy-six.

Although I had no prior interest in researching my family lineage, my grandmother's sister, Lucille Stacy-Smith had always intrigued me. You see, many of the conversations you read in the Fiona Quinn Mysteries are actual conversations I've had with my grandma. I remember these little chats as if we had talked just last week. Fiona's recollected conversation with Grandma Ev in chapter two was, in fact, a genuine dialogue Gram and I had about her sister many, *many* years ago.

So, was this tête-à-tête I had with my grandmother the inspiration for *Mambo and Murder's* storyline?

No.

Actually, a belated mail delivery was my inspiration—rather, I should say, wrongly delivered and late-to-find mail. You see, I had found a bag of discarded magazines, brochures, etc. in an extra bedroom in my home. When I went to throw them away, an envelope fell out of a sales brochure. It was most obvious by the postmark, and a glittery Christmas sticker on the back of the envelope the card was a Christmas card that had been sent out approximately five years earlier.

Yeah, I hadn't cleaned out the closet in that room for quite some time—don't judge.

Anyway, the card was addressed to someone I did not know, at an address I did not recognize—not even in my zip code. The card had a "forever" stamp on it, so I mailed it out immediately. Like my grandmother, I keep Christmas cards I believe to be the last card I've received from important people in my life. I wanted to make sure this card made it to its destination—even if it was five years late. After all, how was I to know if this was the last Christmas card the person would have received from a parent, a sibling, or a grandparent?

As I slipped the belated Christmas card into the mailbox, I immediately thought, *so, what would happen if Fiona began receiving mail from years past?* And Immediately, I thought of Lucille. Suddenly, a second or parallel storyline for Mambo and Murder began to hatch inside my head.

Lucille was sibling number six in the extensive Stacy brood and she was eight years older than my grandmother. During our conversation many years ago, my grandmother *hinted* that Lucille had spent time in a mental institution. I could not find any such evidence in my research to support Gram's subtle innuendo. In fact, finding anything at all on Lucille was nearly impossible. Perhaps there was so little information because she died shortly after giving birth to her third child, Blanche. Lucille was twenty-five when she passed due to bronchial pneumonia. The death certificate I discovered did not specify where Lucille met her demise, only that she died in the Pittsburgh area.

As I was writing, *Mambo and Murder*, I was beginning to feel a little guilty for the possible untruths I was eluding to with Lucille and with Wilbur in *Merry Murder*— no, he did not play Santa at the mall and, again, he was not murdered. But then it struck me: Wait a minute. These people are deceased and have been gone for a *very* long time. Essentially, I am taking them (through my storytelling) on one more adventure—an adventure I'm sure they'd never experienced or, for that matter, imagined in their wildest dreams. I am taking two people who have been forgotten, basically because there is no one alive left to remember them, and I've brought them to readers who loved them, identified with them, and certainly sympathized with them.

In order to stay within the story's present-day timeline, I had to pluck my great uncle and great aunt from the decades in which they existed and move them forward *many* years. Wilbur actually lived from 1894-1976 and Lucille's short life spanned 1904-1929. Lucille's husband, Edward Smith and all three of their children, Edward, Richard (otherwise known as Dick), and

Blanche are deceased as well. My grandmother, Evelyn, passed away in 1991. The last and youngest of the Stacy siblings, Ruth, died in 2003 (Ruth is *mentioned* in *Merry Murder*).

Yes, writing the Fiona Quinn Mysteries has awakened something inside of me that laid dormant for a long time. Please remember, the Fiona Quinn Mysteries are a work of fiction—with a few people from my family tree who have been roused for one more escapade.

Enjoy other books from the Fiona Quinn Mysteries:

Murder on Pointe
Merry Murder
Waves of Murder
Tastes Like Murder
Good Luck to Murder

Short stories from Fiona Quinn Quick Mysteries:

Banking on a Murder
Harriet's Heist

All of the Fiona Quinn full-length mysteries are now available on audiobook. The stories are narrated by Maren Swenson-Waxenberg—she has become the voice of Fiona Quinn and brings the characters to life in such a wonderful style.

For more information and to listen to audio excerpts from the Fiona Quinn Mysteries, please visit my website: www.csmcdonaldbooks.com

Made in the USA
Middletown, DE
02 November 2021